Romeo and Juliet

– novel –

PAUL ILLIDGE

Creber Monde

For Barbara Chilcott Somers

Published by Creber Monde Entier
265 Port Union, 15-532
Toronto, ON M1C 4Z7 Canada
(416) 286-3988 1-866-631-4440 toll free
www.crebermonde.com

Distributed by Independent Publishers Group
814 North Franklin Street
Chicago, Illinois 60610 USA
(312) 337-0747 (312) 337-5985 fax
www.ipgbook.com
frontdesk@ipgbook.com

Design by Derek Chung Tiam Fook
Communications by JAG Business Services Inc.
Printed and bound in Canada by Hignell Book Printing, Winnipeg, Manitoba

Library and Archives Canada Cataloguing in Publication

Illidge, Paul
Romeo and Juliet / prose translation by Paul Illidge.

(The Shakespeare novels)
ISBN 0-9686347-1-0

I. Title. II. Series: Illidge, Paul. Shakespeare novels.

PR2878.R65I45 2005 C813'.54 C2005-901590-X

Romeo and Juliet

Text of the First Folio 1623

Characters

Escalus	*Prince of Verona*
Mercutio	a *young gentleman and kinsman to the Prince, friend of Romeo's*
Paris	*a noble young kinsman to the Prince*
Page	*to Paris*
Montague	*head of family feuding with the Capulets*
Lady Montague	*his wife*
Romeo	*Montague's son*
Benvolio	*Montague's nephew and friend of Romeo and Mercutio*
Abraham	*a servant to Montague*
Balthasar	*Romeo's servant*
Capulet	*head of family feuding with the Montagues*
Lady Capulet	*his wife*
Juliet	*Capulet's daughter*
Tybalt	*Lady Capulet's nephew*
Cousin Capulet	*an old gentleman*
Nurse	*a Capulet servant, Juliet's foster-mother*
Peter	*a Capulet servant assisting the Nurse*
Sampson	
Gregory	
Anthony	*of the Capulet household*
Potpan	
Serving Men	
Friar Laurence	*Franciscan monks*
Friar John	
Apothecary	*of Mantua*
Three Musicians	*Simon Catling, Hugh Rebeck, James Soundpost*
Chorus	

Chorus

Two noble families in fair Verona, where the story is set, revive their long standing hostility towards each other so that the whole city is embroiled, almost to the point of civil war.

Amid this bitter conflict, two children from the feuding households fall in love and then, tragically, commit suicide, which finally puts an end to their parents' destructive hatred.

This disturbing story of doomed youth trying to make love work in spite of their parents' violent objection, will occupy the stage for the next two hours.

So listen carefully: what we haven't told you here, we hope you will behold in this play of ours.

—— ♥ ——

Armed with swords and small shields, Gregory and Sampson, two young Capulet supporters, are roaming a public square in 16th century Verona. The apprehensive looks on their faces suggest they're ready for trouble to crop up at any moment. Their conversation is not just about how easily, but about how eagerly they can be motivated to get into a fight, especially if it involves anyone named Montague.

No sooner have they acknowledged this, than they spot Abraham and Balthasar, two Montague supporters, up ahead. Gregory immediately draws his sword and orders Sampson to do the same.

Excited yet nervous, they agree to let the Montagues start the fight, which is in keeping with their belligerent attitude: it's not a matter of *if* it will happen, but *when*.

Gregory says he'll just make a face as they pass each other to see what that stirs up. His confidence boosted, Sampson says he will make a rude gesture once they get closer.

Face to face now, Sampson follows through and gestures at Abraham and Balthasar.

"Are you making that rude gesture at me?" Abraham inquires.

"I'm making a rude gesture," Sampson allows.

"But are you making it at my friend and me?"

Not the brightest boy around, Sampson looks to Gregory for advice. He shakes his head 'no' as the four young men approach each other, exchanging menacing glares.

"No I'm not," Sampson replies following Gregory's cue. "Like I said, I'm not making a rude gesture at *you*. I'm just making a rude gesture."

"Do you have a problem with that?" Gregory speaks up.

Abraham snickers. "A problem? No, I don't have a problem with *that*."

"Because if you do have a problem with that, maybe we should do something about it. After all, I work for as good a man as you do."

"He's certainly no better," Abraham sneers.

"But I'd say he was," Gregory taunts. "And here comes one of his relatives now."

"Yes, I would definitely say ours is better than theirs," Sampson boasts.

"I doubt that," says Abraham.

"So, draw your swords and let's find out!"

The swordfighters rattle and clash until Benvolio, a Montague cousin, charges into the fray.

"Stop it!" he screams and with deft sword work forces them to put down their weapons, just as a Capulet cousin named Tybalt arrives on the scene, draws his sword and confronts Benvolio.

"Prepare to die, Benvolio!"

"I was trying to break them up! Put your sword away or use it to try and help me!"

"I'll use it, but not to make peace! I hate that word, I hate the Montagues, and I hate you! Take that you coward" Tybalt shouts and attacks Benvolio so ruthlessly he has no choice but to defend himself.

Within moments the melee has heated up, attracting a crowd of onlookers, some wielding clubs and sticks as they wade into the conflict.

"Down with the Capulets!"

"Down with the Montagues!"

Alerted to the upheaval, the distinguished Lord Capulet directs his entourage toward the noisy throng in the square. "Give me my long sword!" he cries.

"You mean a crutch!" Lady Capulet shrieks as she restrains her elderly husband.

"What do you want with a sword…."

"I said my *sword!*" Capulet storms, although more out of pride, bravado and old habit than any convincing belief he will make a difference to what is going on. "Old Montague over there has *his* weapon out!" he protests to his wife.

"You villain Capulet!" Lord Montague cries over the clamor of the fighting crowd, trying to break free from his own wife's grasp. "Let me go, for heaven's sake – "

No sooner has he done so, however, than armed soldiers clear the way for Escalus, Prince of Verona.

"Rebellious subjects! Enemies of peace!" he thunders. "Throw down your weapons and listen to me!" He glares with fierce authority at the Montague and Capulet factions as his men subdue the jostling mob. "You're like a pack of wild animals tearing at each other as if fountains of spilled blood are going to quench the despicable anger that burns inside you, regardless of the painful consequences. I'm giving you my final warning about this senseless violence you've inflicted on the city, rioting repeatedly over nothing but bitter words exchanged by you Capulet, and you Montague.

"Your mutual hatred has infected everyone in Verona; even the eldest and most revered citizens have taken sides. Therefore, I declare that if there's one more incident of fighting or brawling, both of you shall be put to death."

Furious that the Prince has intervened, the Lords Montague and Capulet and their followers refuse to meet his eyes.

"I order you all to disperse immediately. Capulet, you come with me now, and Montague, you present yourself at the Freetown court this afternoon so I can make my position clear to you: the penalty for any disturbance is death. Now, be gone...."

Everyone obeys until in a few minutes only Lord and Lady Montague, and Benvolio remain behind.

"Did you see who started this, nephew?" Lord Montague inquires.

Benvolio explains to his uncle that the Capulet servants were well into the fight by the time he came along. "I was trying to get both sides to stop when Tybalt charged up with his sword waving and attacked me. While I did my best to fend him off, more and more people joined in on either side until the Prince came and made us stop, as you saw."

"Where's Romeo, for goodness sake," Lady Montague worries. "Have you seen him today?" she asks Benvolio. "Thank heavens he wasn't involved in this ruckus."

Benvolio informs his aunt that about an hour before dawn that morning he got up and went for a walk because he couldn't sleep. He was over near the sycamore grove on the west side of the city.

"At one point I saw Romeo and was heading over to him when he noticed me coming and ducked into the woods. Since I felt like being left alone too, I didn't bother to go after him."

"He seems to go there most mornings now," Lord Montague offers with a somber frown, "letting his tears mix with the dew, adding his gloomy sighs to the remnant clouds of night—until the rising sun flings open the curtains of day, at which point he races home to his room and shuts the blinds to keep himself in continual darkness." He shakes his head in concern. "Such behavior never turns out well, to be sure; when you don't know the cause, you can't help with the cure ."

Benvolio nods. "You have no idea what he's suffering from..."

"None."

"And you can't pry it out of him?"

"I've tried, believe me. My friends have too. But Romeo's feelings, false or true, are closely guarded secrets he keeps to himself. If we had an inkling of how the sorrow began, we'd do everything possible to understand."

"There he is now. Move off a ways; I'll see if I can uncover the source of his malaise."

"It would be a welcome relief if you could get through to him."

He and Lady Montague hurry out of sight, but not before Romeo spots them across the square.

"Good morning, cousin!" Benvolio calls as he approaches Romeo.

"Is the day so young?" Romeo asks without looking up.

"Barely nine o'clock."

Romeo sighs wearily. "Sad hours seem long. Was that my father who ran off so fast?"

"It was. But tell me, why do the hours seem so long?"

"Not having that which would make them seem short."

"You're in love then?"

"Out."

"Of love?"

"Out of favor with the one I love."

"Alas that love which you saw as so gentle, should turn out to be so cruel, so unkind."

"Alas that even without eyes, love can follow a path of its own choosing. Where shall we dine? O my! Was there a quarrel here? No, don't tell me – I know what happened. It had to do with hate, and love as well. Why must love be so brawling, hate so loving? How can something so strong be created from nothing. It's such heavy lightness, such serious vanity, a misshapen chaos of appealing forms. Feather of lead, bright smoke, cold fire, sick health, waking sleep that is not what it appears to be. This love I feel that can't feel love. Why are you laughing?"

"I'm not. I'm crying."

"What on earth for?"

"To see your good heart suffering such oppression."

"And causing even more transgression – my own griefs are

weighing me down but they will grow heavier when they distress you. This compassion you're showing only adds more sadness to the over abundance I already have. Love is a smoke made with the fume of sighs; once it clears, the fire sparkles in lovers' eyes. When upset, it's a sea brimming with lovers' tears. What else could it be? A tactful madness, a choking bitterness, a preserving sweetness? Farewell, cousin."

"Wait, I'll go along with you. Don't leave me here alone."

"Of course. But I'm lost in my own thoughts. I'm not really myself. Romeo is somewhere else."

"Reach into your sadness and tell me who it is you love"

"What, complain about it to you?"

"Complain? No, just tell me who."

"Tell a man suffering a sickness to draw up his will? The word alone could make him more ill. Sadly, cousin, I do love a woman."

"I hit the bull's eye then," Benvolio winks cheerfully.

"You're an excellent marksman, yes. I'm in love with a beautiful girl."

"An obvious target – they're the easiest to hit, cousin."

"Well, in that hit you miss; she won't let herself be struck by Cupid's dart, she has a mind as determined as Diana's, goddess of the hunt. Love bounces off her like an arrow from a child's toy bow. She refuses to become romantically involved, won't submit to force or be won over by all the gold in the world. Indeed, she is rich in beauty yet poor in that when she dies her treasure will die with her."

"So she has sworn to remain chaste?"

"She has, to live without earthly love – depriving future generations from inheriting her beauty. She is too lovely, too honest for her own good. A quest for spiritual bliss? That's what casts me in despair like this. She has renounced love, and made me one of the living dead by that vow, one who can merely relate her story now."

"Listen to me: stop thinking about her."

"What? How can I stop thinking?"

"By opening your eyes to the beauty of other girls."

"She would still stand out as the most exquisite." Romeo reflects for a moment and then continues. "Even wearing a mask, we know a woman's beauty is still there, Benvolio. The same as one who is struck blind can never forget how wonderful it was having eyesight. Show me a girl who is attractive – what purpose does her beauty serve, other than as a reminder that so many others found her beautiful too. Farewell Benvolio. You can't teach me to forget her."

"I'll pay for the lessons to try," Benvolio declares, "although it may leave me in debt when I die!"

— ♥ —

Lord Capulet is talking to Paris, a young nobleman related to the Prince of Verona. Along with one of his servants, Capulet leads the way through crowded medieval streets.

"So Montague will pay the same penalty as I do if there's another altercation – you would think men as old as we are could keep the peace."

"Especially since you both have such honorable reputations," Paris points out. "It's a shame you've been enemies for so long."

Noticing Lord Capulet, people step aside as he passes by.

"By the way, my lord," Paris says, raising his voice to be heard above the din of the crowd, "what is your opinion of my proposal?"

"I'll repeat what I said before, Paris. My daughter is still unfamiliar with the ways of the world. She's not even fourteen yet. I think with two more summers on her side, Juliet will be ready to become your bride."

"Some girls her age are married and becoming mothers."

"Forced out of childhood too soon! Which is fine for others, but death has robbed me of all my children except her. She means the world to me. Woo her gently, Paris. My permission is a mere part of what the girl decides in her heart; I will just lend a concurring voice to whoever Juliet makes her choice."

Lord Capulet stops abruptly and opens up a paper scroll he is carrying. It contains an extensive list of handwritten names.

"Tonight I'm holding my annual April celebration for old and valued friends, of which you are certainly one. You're very welcome to attend – the more the merrier, isn't that what they say?"

Satisfied that the invitation list is complete, he closes the scroll and hands it to his servant.

"Why don't you come by the house?" he says, inviting Paris to the soirée. "You'll be amazed to see how brightly young women can light up a Spring night. You and the other lusty young men can behold the blossoming flowers, as it were. Perhaps seeing Juliet among the bevy of beauties, you'll glimpse someone who merits further consideration, as it were," he winks.

Capulet takes Paris by the arm then turns to his servant.

"Go through Verona, sir, and locate the people whose names are written there. Tell them we're looking forward to the pleasure of their company tonight."

He leads Paris off, leaving the servant on his own. The simple fellow stares blankly at the list of names on the scroll. "Locate the people whose names are written here," he frowns, repeating Capulet's instructions. "They say the shoemaker should be able to handle a yardstick, the tailor his wooden foot mount, the fisher his pallette and the painter his nets. I'm supposed to find those people whose names are written here, but first I'll have to find someone who can tell me what names the writer has put down – someone who knows how to read." Jostled by the throng of people passing by, he gazes helplessly in one direction after another. Suddenly his face brightens. "Ahhh!" he cries, "in the nick of time!"

Benvolio and Romeo are approaching, deeply engrossed in conversation. Judging by their fine clothes, they are more sophisticated than most of the other people around so Capulet's servant heads toward them.

"Relax," Benvolio tells Romeo. "As one fire burns out another one is coming to life. One pain decreases the moment another begins. Deep grief is cured the instant there's a different cause for suffering. Get a new infection in your eye, the rank poison of a former one will die."

"Plantain leaf is excellent for that," Romeo says obscurely.

"For what?"

"For a cracked shin."

"Romeo, are you losing your mind?"

"No, but I feel as if I'm shackled like one who is. Imprisoned. Starved. Whipped. Tortured. And – evening, good fellow," he says as Capulet's servant confronts them.

"Well, a pleasant good evening to you too, sir. Begging your pardon, but, do you by any chance know how to read?"

"Read? My own miserable fortune."

The servant throws Romeo a questioning look. "Well, even if you didn't go to school, can you read things by looking at them?"

Romeo puzzles over the question, keeping his eyes off Benvolio, who suppresses a mischievous smile.

"It depends whether I recognize the letters and the idiom."

Confused by this explanation, the servant takes Romeo's answer for a 'no'.

"Well, thanks for your honesty then. Have a good night."

He moves to step between them and continue on his way but Romeo holds him back.

"Hang on, my friend. I know how to read."

Smiling, the servant hands over the scroll.

"*Signor Martino, his wife and daughters,*" Romeo reads. "*Count Anselm and his beauteous sisters. The widow Utruvio. Signor Placentio and his lovely nieces. Mercutio and his brother Valentine. My uncle Capulet, his wife and daughters. My fair niece Rosaline and Livia. Signor Valentino and his cousin Tybalt. Lucio and the vivacious Helena.* An impressive group. Now where would they be off to?"

"Up."

"To dine somewhere?"

"At our house."

"Whose?"

"My master's!"

"All right. I should have asked you that before."

"No need to ask. I'll tell you," the servant says helpfully. "My master is the great rich Capulet, and if you don't happen to belong to the house of Montague, you're welcome to come by for a glass of wine."

He takes back his scroll, bids them a good evening and hurries on his way.

Benvolio takes Romeo by the shoulders. "The fair Rosaline – the one you love – will be at Capulet's party! Along with plenty of Verona's finest! Why don't we stop by so you can look at her alongside some girls I can point out – some who will make you see your swan as a crow, I have no doubt."

"To think anyone could be more fair than my love is sacrilege. There has never been her equal, not since time began, and that's a fact."

"No it's not. You decided she was ravishing because you had no one to compare her with. But if you hold Rosaline up to those who'll be at Capulet's, I guarantee you'll change your mind."

"I'll go along, though only one thing will affect what I see – the rapturous sight of Rosaline, the splendor of her beauty."

—— ♥ ——

Lady Capulet moves quickly through an upstairs hallway searching for her daughter Juliet while Nurse, who has looked after Juliet since she was a baby, opens and closes doors to the rooms farther down the corridor.

"Where's my daughter?" Lady Capulet demands. "Find her and bring her to me if you would."

"Sweetheart!" Nurse calls. "Where are you, my dear? Juliet!"

The girl appears out of nowhere and creeps up behind Nurse, playfully putting her hands over Nurse's eyes.

"Who is it?"

"Your mother!" Nurse says, shaking her head.

Juliet lowers her hands and gives Nurse a fond hug. "Here I am, madam! What's wrong?" she asks her mother.

"Well, I'll tell you. Nurse, would you give us a minute? We have a somewhat private matter to discuss."

Nurse turns to leave but Lady Capulet reconsiders.

"No, come back! I wasn't thinking. You should hear this too. I'm sure you realize my daughter has reached the age in a girl's life – "

"I can tell you her age right down to the very hour," Nurse interjects.

"As she's about to turn fourteen –"

"I'll bet fourteen teeth – even though there's but four left – she is definitely about to turn fourteen. How long is it to August the first?"

"Two weeks and a few days –"

"Give or take, the night of July thirty-first she'll be exactly fourteen. Susan and she – bless her poor soul – were the same age. Well, Susan is with God now. She was too good for me that girl. But, as I said, the night of the thirty-first she'll be turning fourteen, yes she will. Oh, I remember it like it was yesterday. Eleven years ago we had the earthquake and I was weaning her – I'll never forget that. More than all the other days of the year. I had laid some bitter-green leaves on my breast while I was feeding her in the sun beside the garden wall. Lord Capulet and you had gone to Mantua – my, how I remember things.... But, as I was saying, when the little one tasted the bitter-green on my nipple it was really something, pretty fool.... Watching her make a face and pull back from my breast. When the ground started shaking I didn't need to be told to get out of there."

Nurse crosses her arms over her chest before continuing.

"It's eleven years since then. She was already standing up – she would have been running all around if she'd had her way. Why, just the day before she fell and bumped her forehead. And my husband – bless the man, he was such a character – he lifts her up. 'Now' says he, 'did you fall on your wee face? Before you know it you'll be falling over on your back, do you know that Jule?' And on my word the little thing stops crying and blurts out 'Yes.'

"To think how Fate works. If I live to be a thousand I'll never forget it. 'Do you know that Jule?' he says. And the silly girl, she stops and says 'Yes' right back to him."

"Enough of this," Lady Capulet declares impatiently. "Hush, Nurse."

"Yes, madam. But it is funny she would just stop crying and say 'Yes'. And I swear the bump on her head was the size of a goose egg, and she was wailing away. 'Yes,' says my husband, 'fell on your wee face did you? Well, you'll be falling on your back when you come of age, won't you Jule? When she stops and cries 'Yes –'"

"All right, Nurse," cries Juliet.

"I'll hold my peace then. As God is my witness you were the prettiest baby I ever had the joy of nursing. That I should live to see your wedding day – my wish will have come true."

"Which is what I wanted to discuss," says Lady Capulet. "Tell me, Juliet. What are your thoughts on marriage?"

"It is an honor I can't even imagine."

"An honor," Nurse says. "If I wasn't the only one who nursed you, I'd say you picked up some decent wisdom feeding off me."

"Well, think about it now," Lady Capulet instructs. "Younger girls than you here in Verona, ones of considerable social standing, have already become mothers. If I'm not mistaken, I was the same age when I had you. So, returning to the point. The valiant Paris is asking for your hand – "

"Oh, young lady! What a catch! The perfect man!"

"Verona's most desirable bachelor," Lady Capulet points out.

"Desirable! I'll say he's desirable!" Nurse exclaims.

"What do you think?" Lady Capulet puts the question to Juliet. "Can you see yourself loving someone like him? Tonight you'll have a chance to meet him at the party. It wouldn't hurt to peruse the pages, so to speak. See how well composed his features are, which tells you about the quality of the contents within – particularly the eyes. Like a freshly printed book, a suitable cover tops off what's inside – remember the sea is made more beautiful by having beautiful fish within it. What I'm saying is that a good book derives as much glory from fine binding as a well-told story. You would reap the benefits of a prestigious life, and enlarge your status by becoming his wife."

"A woman is enlarged by her man, that's for sure," Nurse grins.

"What do you have to say, could you accept someone like Paris?"

"I'll look forward to liking him if he is to my liking. But I won't commit myself to the man without your permission, madam."

A flustered serving man rushes to Lady Capulet's side.

"Madam, the guests are arriving, supper is being served, people are calling for you and asking for the young lady. In the kitchen they're cursing you, Nurse, because there's still a lot to do. I have to get back and begin serving, so please come as quickly as you can."

"Very well. Juliet, Count Paris awaits."

"Off you go, then!" Nurse cries. "A girl is lost who hesitates!"

—— ♥ ——

Their torches blazing, Romeo, Benvolio, their friend Mercutio, and half a dozen other young men in masks and costumes, make their way through a dark street toward the Capulet house.

"Should we introduce ourselves with the regular formalities, or just go right in?" Romeo inquires.

"That sort of thing is so old-fashioned," Benvolio complains. "We don't need to put on elaborate charades – blindfolded Cupids carrying fake bows and arrows, scaring girls with our rowdiness, acting out comedy routines. What they see is what they get. We'll have one or two dances and then be on our way."

"Let me carry one of the torches. I'm not feeling very sociable."

"No, Romeo. You're dancing whether you like it or not," Mercutio tells him.

"I don't think so. You've got your dancing shoes with light soles on; my soul drags me down like a lead weight so I can barely move."

"You're a lover!" Mercutio shouts. "Borrow Cupid's wings and soar away from your burdens."

"I've been struck by one of his arrows, Mercutio. I've hit bottom and I can't get up I ache so badly – it's like I'm in a boat that's overloaded and starting to sink."

"Well, you'll drown if you're not careful. And since when did such a pleasurable thing become so complicated?"

"Love pleasurable? Not for me. It's fierce, sharp and tormenting, like thorns are constantly pricking me."

"If love is tormenting you, my friend, start tormenting love. Prick love if it's pricking you, and send it back where it belongs. Give me a bag to put my mask in. What do I care who sees my ugliness? A pair of bushy eyebrows will do the trick."

"All right, let's knock and go in," Benvolio urges. "And let's get the dancing underway!"

"A torch for me," Romeo says quietly. "Let the carefree and the light of heart do the dancing. As my grandfather used to say, 'I'm a bystander now that my dancing days are done.'"

"Done? Enough of that!" Mercutio hollers. "We'll yank you out of the quicksand where love is pulling you under. Come on, we're wasting time."

"No, we're not," Romeo objects.

"I only meant that the longer we delay, the lower the flames will burn. We can deliberate the pro's and con's all night, or we can trust to our instincts and just join in the fun."

"If our intentions in going to the party are honorable, fine. But otherwise we shouldn't put in an appearance."

"And why not?" Mercutio demands.

"I had a dream earlier tonight," Romeo says.

Mercutio laughs. "So did I!"

"What was yours about?"

"That dreamers often lie."

"In sleep, dreams are true."

"Oh. I see Queen Mab has been visiting you. The fairies midwife? Who appears the size of an agate stone on the ring of the alderman's baby finger. Drawn by a little team of mites over people's noses while they sleep, her chariot is an empty hazel nut shell made by the squirrels, coachmakers to the fairies from time immemorial. The wheel spokes made of spinners' legs, the cover from wings of grasshoppers. Her reins are the smallest spiders' webs, her bridles of moonlight's watery beams, her whip of tiny cricket's bone, her driver the tiniest, gray-coated gnat. In this sprightly manner she gallops at night through lovers' brains to make them dream of love. Over courtiers' knees, who dream of bowing before the King. Over lawyers' fingers, itching to have their fees. Over women's lips who only dream of sweet young kisses –"

"Hold on, Mercutio!" Romeo protests. "You're talking nonsense!"

"You're right. I'm talking about dreams, children of an idle brain put together from nothing but wishful fantasies. Thinner than air, shifting like the wind –"

"Speaking of which, your windiness is blowing us away from our destination. Supper is nearly over – we're going to arrive too late."

"No, I'm afraid we could be early," Romeo says gravely. "I have a strange feeling about all of this. An omen hanging in the stars, ready to fall this night with dire consequences…where an unhappy life like my own could be lost to an untimely death. But it's out of my hands, I suppose; on, lusty gentlemen."

"Let's go!" Benvolio shouts to the others.

— ♥ —

Their trays stacked with plates and bowls, two serving men squeeze through a crush of masked and costumed people on their way to the kitchen in the Capulet house.

"Why isn't Potpan helping us with the tables?" one of them demands. "He's a loafer. Nothing but a loafer! if you ask me."

"When everything's left to be done by the two of us, it's hardly fair," the other man replies.

"Clear the dishes!" the first man calls to the other servants. "Remove the platters! Get to work on those cutting boards! You there, save me a piece of marzipan! And do me a favor. Have the porter get Susan Grindstone and Nell out here on the double! Anthony! Potpan!

"At your service," Potpan pipes up, but in a less than energetic voice.

"You're needed in the great chamber," says the first serving man. "Immediately!"

"We can't be in two places at once," a fourth man adds. "Cheerio, boys! Better get a move on, he who lives the longest takes it all!"

Capulet and Lady Capulet move across the colorfully decorated, spacious room enjoying the lively celebration. Juliet and her cousin Tybalt follow close behind, along with an entourage of well-dressed gentlemen and their exquisitely gowned gentlewomen.

"Welcome, one and all," Capulet says addressing various friends. "Gentlemen, the women are eager for more dancing. Ladies, which one of you won't grace them with the favor of your charms? She who holds back must have something wrong with her legs. Must I lead the way myself? Welcome, gentlemen!" He has noticed Mercutio, Benvolio and the other masquers. "I remember the days when I went to all the masques – when I whispered enticing tidbits into a fair lady's ear. Pity those times are behind me now. Pity…. But you're all welcome here this evening. Gentlemen, please join us! Musicians play! Make way, make way. Let's have some room! Don't be shy, girls!"

The musicians promptly strike up a festive melody and the dancing begins in earnest.

"More candles in here, you fools!" Capulet calls to his servants. "Move the tables aside! Put out the fire, the room is too hot."

He shows his elderly cousin Capulet to a chair and the two men sit down.

"The presence of these maskers is certainly a pleasant surprise. How long is it since we did that kind of thing?"

"I'd say thirty years or so," cousin Capulet allows.

"Not thirty!" Capulet objects. "It was about the time of Lucentio's wedding. That's only coming up on twenty-five."

"No no, it's more than that. Lucentio himself is only thirty years old."

"That's not right. Seems to me he was just a gangly boy a few years ago…."

On the far side of the room, Romeo threads his way among the party guests. A passing servant offers him something from the dessert tray he is carrying, but Romeo declines. The air filled with the din of music and conversation, he speaks into the servant's ear.

"Who is the lady on the arm of that noble gentleman?"

"I don't know, sir."

"O, she could teach the torches to burn bright. She seems to hang upon the dark of night like a rich jewel in an African ear – beauty too rich for use, for earth too dear. So seems a snow white dove sitting with crows the way this lady among her fellows shows. The dance is done – I'll watch where she comes to stand, and touching hers, make blessed my rough hand. Did my heart love till now? Deny it, sight: for never have I seen true beauty till this night."

"I know that voice. It belongs to a Montague." Tybalt, Lord

Capulet's nephew, glares over at Romeo. "Bring me my sword," he snaps at the boy who accompanies him. "How dare he show his mocking face here among us? I swear on the tombs of my family kin, killing him will be no sin."

"Tybalt! What on earth is going on?" Capulet demands when he notices the boy handing Tybalt a sword.

"That man is a Montague, uncle. Our lifelong enemy. Here to show his scorn for our festivities."

"Isn't that Romeo?"

"It is," Tybalt snipes bitterly.

"Let's leave him alone. He's minding his own business, and as a matter of fact I've heard around town that he's a very respectable and personable young man. For goodness sake, I would never be seen harming him in my own house. Perhaps you could just ignore him. That is what I recommend, so wipe the frown off your face this instant. It doesn't fit with such an occasion."

"It fits when someone like him passes himself off as one of your guests. I can't ignore that."

"But you will," Capulet insists, "you will, young man. Whose house is this, after all? Do you want to cause a scene and have my guests fleeing for the door?"

"It's intolerable, uncle."

"Now now, Tybalt. Sometimes I find your insolence a little intolerable. There's no need for anyone to get hurt. But I think I see – you always like to contradict me, don't you?" He realizes people are applauding a gentleman who's recited a short verse.

"Well said, my friend! You really can be exasperating sometimes," he declares, turning back to Tybalt. "Now, be quiet or – more light! more candles! – or I'll make you be quiet. Cheers, my friends!" Capulet calls and scurries off to bid farewell to some departing guests.

"I'll let things be for now," Tybalt sneers, "but this won't be the end of it. I'll let things be. But when the time comes, I'll make sure he pays for what he's done to me."

Romeo comes up from behind Juliet and surprises her.

"If I profane with my unworthy hand this holy shrine, the reason would be this: my lips, two blushing pilgrims, ready stand to smooth their roughness with a tender kiss."

"Good pilgrim," Juliet smiles, "you do blame your hands too much, which mannerly devotion shows in this; for saints have hands that pilgrims long to touch, and palm to palm is how such pilgrims kiss."

"Have saints not lips as holy pilgrims do?"

"Yes, pilgrim, but lips they use in prayer."

"O then, dear saint, let lips do what hands do and pray: Take mine, lest faith become despair."

"Saints will not move, they wait for prayer's sake."

"Then move not, while my prayer's effect I take," he whispers and kisses her. "Thus from my lips, with yours, my sin's removed."

"But have my lips the sin that they have took?"

"Sin from my lips? O promise now be proved – give me my sin back again."

He kisses her once more.

"You kiss by passion's book!"

"Madam!" cries Nurse, bustling vigorously up to Juliet. "Your mother wants a word."

"Who is her mother?" Romeo asks as Juliet hurries off, glancing excitedly back at him.

Nurse looks him up and down. "Only the lady of the house. And a fine, upstanding lady too. I nursed her daughter, the one you were just talking to. Let me tell you, young man. He that can lay his hands on that young girl will never want for money."

"Is she a Capulet? How can this be. My life at the mercy of my worst enemy."

Benvolio arrives and grabs Romeo by the arm. "Come on, we're going. The fun's over."

"I was afraid of that. What am I going to do?"

"No, gentlemen!" Capulet protests. "Don't leave, we have more treats being prepared." Benvolio whispers in his ear. "Is that right? Why then, I do thank you for dropping by. Good night! Some torches here! Probably for the best. It's growing late. I should be off to bed."

Juliet watches people as they are leaving.

"Nurse, who is that gentleman over there?"

"The son and heir of old Tiberio."

"What about the one just going out the door?"

"Hmm. I think his name's Petruchio."

"And he that's right behind him, the one who wouldn't dance?"

"I don't know him."

"Could you quickly find out? If he's married my grave will become my wedding bed."

Nurse scurries away and returns a moment later.

"His name is Romeo," she tells Juliet, "the only son of Montague, your father's great enemy."

"My only love sprung from my only hate," she sighs wistfully. "Meeting him before knowing him, knowing him too late; how horrible the thought of love to me, when I must love a loathèd enemy."

"What's this? What's this?" Nurse cries, noticing the sad look on Juliet's face.

"A poem I learned from someone I was dancing with," Juliet replies.

"Juliet!" A woman's voice calls from the next room.

"All right, all right! Let's go and get ready for bed," Nurse says, nudging Juliet. "The guests have all gone home."

Chorus

*Now old desires pass away and young affections
strive to take their place; that fair face for whom love
yearned to die, whom Juliet so readily adored,
is now to be forbidden.*

*Though Romeo is loved at last and eager so
to love again (and both bewitched by one another's
looks), his lover's claim he now is forced to lay
before his family's mighty foe – love snatched
away just when it seemed the prize was his!*

*As an enemy he might never have the chance to tell
her what his heart now feels, as lovers long to do,
but even less at liberty is Juliet to meet her love for
secret rendezvous. Yet passion gives them power,
and time the means to meet: bitter anger overcome,
old feuds by love made sweet.*

"How can I go forward when my heart is still there…?" Romeo
asks as he wanders aimlessly down a dark, deserted street after leaving

the Capulet party. He trudges a few steps farther and then abruptly stops. "Turn back my body, and find your very soul!"

Not a moment's hesitation, he wheels around and heads off the way he came, just as Benvolio and Mercutio, coming from a different direction, round the corner up ahead.

"Romeo! My cousin Romeo! Romeo!" Benvolio calls at the top of his voice, but to no avail.

"He's smart to have taken himself home to bed," says Mercutio.

"He ran this way and leapt that orchard wall. Yell, Mercutio. Come on."

"No. I'm going to bring him to life before your very eyes. Romeo! Your Moodiness! Sir Passion! Madman! Lover! Show me what it's like to be a sigh; let me hear some poetry, boy, and I'll be satisfied. Use the phrase "Ay me!" why don't you. Make 'love' rhyme with 'dove'. Put in a word to Old Lady Venus – maybe a nickname for her hopelessly blind son and heir: Abraham J. Cupid, the one with such good aim that King Cophetua ended up making love to a helpless beggar maid."

Still no response, Mercutio changes tactics.

"He doesn't hear me! Doesn't answer! Plays at hiding! The monkey's dead, but I must bring him back to life! So. By the light in Rosalind's eyes, her perfect face, her scarlet lips, curving waist, quivering thighs – and all that there adjacent lies – I order you to appear before us: NOW!"

"If he hears you, it will only make him angry."

"This won't make him angry. It would make him angry if I put forward the fantasy of a naked man, and let him stand while I had Rosalind open wide and make him disappear. That would anger him! My conjuring spell was poetic. I only made it in Rosalind's name to see if I could rouse him."

"Never mind about it now. He's decided to hide somewhere in the trees so he can be alone with the night. He's blinded by love so what better place is there than darkness?"

"If love really is blind," Mercutio ponders, "how can we ever be sure it's with the right person...? There he'll be, sitting under an apple tree, wishing fair Rosaline were like the ripe red fruit just waiting to be picked. Oh Romeo, if only she were – if only she were an open bum, and you a prickly pear! Good night Romeo. I'm going home to my baby crib, it's too cold for one as tender as me. Off we go!"

"Off we go is right. Why waste time looking for someone who doesn't want to be found tonight?"

—— ♥ ——

"He makes fun of things he knows absolutely nothing about...."

Nearby, Romeo comes out from behind a small grove of trees and stares up at the Capulet house. "But wait, what light through yonder window breaks? It is the east and Juliet the rising sun! Arise bright sun and kill the envious moon who has grown sick and pale with grief that you her maid are now far more than she. Her clothes so pale and faded – cast them off. It is my lady, it is my perfect love! If only she could tell. She speaks, yet makes no sound. Why would that be?

"And now her eyes begin expressing – I will answer, just to show her I am here! I am too bold; maybe it's not to me she speaks. Two of the brightest stars in heaven, if called elsewhere, could ask her eyes to twinkle in their place. What if her eyes were there, having left her head? The glow that lights her cheek would put the stars to shame, as daylight does a lamp.

"Her eyes in heaven would through the blackest region stream so bright, that early morning birds would sing and think it were not night. Look at the way she leans her cheek upon her hand. If only I were a glove upon that hand so I could touch that cheek."

"Ah me," she sighs, gazing toward the stars.

"She speaks. Oh do so again bright angel," Romeo urges, "for you are as glorious to this night above my head as a winged messenger from heaven is to the upturned wondering eyes of humans, who in fascination watch him fly among the dark night clouds and sail upon the currents of windy air."

"Oh Romeo, Romeo, why must your name be Romeo? Deny your father and give up your name. Or if you will not, then swear you love me and I will no longer be a Capulet."

"Shall I hear more or speak?"

"It is only your name which is my enemy. You are yourself, not merely a Montague. Besides, what is Montague? It is neither hand nor foot, neither arm nor face nor any other part belonging to a man. Oh be some other name. What's in a name? What we call a rose by any other name would smell the same; so Romeo would too, were his name not Romeo. Let him keep that pure perfection which he owns without that title. Romeo, renounce your name which is no part of you and take all myself."

"I take you at your word! Call me your one and only love and I'll be reborn – I will never be the person known as Romeo again."

"What man is this who eavesdrops late at night outside my room?" Juliet cries in alarm.

"By my name I know not how to tell you who I am: my name, dear saint, is hateful to myself because it is an enemy to you. If down on paper, I would tear it into pieces."

"My ears have only heard a hundred words of what you say, and yet I know the sound. Are you not Romeo, and a Montague?

"I am neither if you dislike them."

"Why have you dared to come here? How did you find your way in? The orchard walls are high and hard to climb, the place your death if someone from my family finds you here."

"With love's light wings I soared above the walls, for barriers made of stone can never hold love out, and anything that love can dream of doing, it will attempt – even your family cannot stop me."

"If you're discovered, they will murder you."

"For me there is more danger in your eye than twenty of their swords – look upon me with favor and I am protected against their hatred

"I would not have them see you here for all the world."

"I have the cloak of darkness to hide myself in, and as long as you love me, I don't care if they find me here. My life would be better ended by their hate this night than by death in years to come not having known your love."

"Who told you how to find this place?"

"Love, who first did prompt me to find out who you were. He

guided me. I loaned him my eyes. And though I am no explorer, if you were farther away than the vast shore in the most distant sea on earth, I would travel there to reach you."

"If it weren't so dark you would see how I am blushing that you heard me speak my thoughts," Juliet confesses. "I would willingly reconsider things I've said; I would gladly take back my words. But so much for the rules of proper etiquette – do you really love me? I know you will say yes, and I will accept that. Yet if you vow that it is so, you could always break your word.

"Gentle Romeo, if you do love me, declare it with all honesty. If you think I'm too easily won over, I'll make mad faces, have temper tantrums, and refuse your affections if it will keep you pursuing me. But others besides you I would not want for anything in the world. The truth is, fair Montague, I am too impulsive and no doubt you think my actions immature, but believe me, I'll prove more worthy than those who have great skill at playing coy. I would have been more reserved all along, except you overheard how passionate I felt before I was aware of it. So forgive me, and please don't take my feelings as a young girl's playful crush."

"Dearest one, by yonder sacred moon that tips the tops of trees with silver light, I swear –"

"Don't swear by the moon – the unreliable moon that changes orbit every month – in case your love proves likewise prone to change."

"What shall I swear by?"

"Don't swear at all. Or if you must, swear by your precious self, which is the god I now worship, for then I will believe you."

"If my heart's true love –"

"Wait! Do not swear, after all. Although I delight in you so much, I can't feel the same about a solemn oath tonight. It is too rash, too unadvised, too sudden – too much like lightning, which disappears before you can say 'Look how it lightens up the sky.' Good night, sweetheart. This bud of love with summer's ripening breeze may bloom by the time we meet again. Good night, good night. As sweet a sleep and gentle rest come to your heart as those that find their place within my breast."

"Must you leave me so unsatisfied?"

"What other satisfaction could you possibly have tonight?"

"A promise that you will love as deeply as I will love you."

"I gave you my promise even before you requested it of me. I wish it were possible to give it again."

"Why, do you want to take it back?"

"No! Just to prove that I mean it by telling you over again. And yet I only wish to give what I already have. The extent of my love is as deep and boundless as the sea. The more I offer, the more of it floods in, filling me with the urge to give you greater amounts each time, and it feels as though this could continue forever. I hear someone coming – dearest love, farewell!"

Nurse calls to Juliet from inside the house.

"In a minute, good Nurse. Sweet Montague be true. Wait here a moment; I'll come right back," Juliet tells him as she returns to her room.

"Oh blessed blessed night – though I fear because it's night this could all just be a dream."

"Dear Romeo, three words to you" says Juliet, reappearing, "and then I have to say adieu. If your intentions toward me are honorable – if marriage is what you are hoping for, send word through the messenger who will come to see you. Convey the details as to time and place for a ceremony and all I have is yours, my love, and at your side I'll stay our whole life long."

"Madam!" Nurse calls in exasperation.

"In a minute! But if there is some other purpose in your mind, then I beg you – "

"Madam!"

"All right, I'm coming – stop right now and leave me with my hurt. Tomorrow I'll send someone – "

"Stay, my soul!"

"A thousand times good night."

"A thousand times worse to crave your light. Love goes toward love like students freed from their books, but love departs from love like students back to school with sorry looks."

Juliet suddenly appears again.

"Romeo! Are you there? If only I could say his name louder, I would shout it till my voice had lost all sound."

"She calls to me – how softly loving whispers in the night air abound."

"Romeo."

"My sweet."

"What time tomorrow should I send for you?"

"Let's say by nine o'clock."

"By nine o'clock it is – though it feels as if that's twenty years away. I can't remember why I called you back – "

"I'll wait until you do."

"Perhaps it was on purpose, just to have you wait while I remember how I love your company."

"And I'll still stay for as long as you still forget, forgetting my own house for yours."

"It's almost morning, I think you should leave, and yet I want you near, like a playful child who keeps her pet on a leash of silken thread to bring it back again, so lovingly jealous is she of its freedom."

"I wish I were that pet."

"If only you could be, but I would kill you from caring for you so much. Good night, good night. Parting is such sweet sorrow that I will say good night until tomorrow."

He watches her go for the last time.

"Sleep inhabit your eyes, peace your breast. If only I were sleep and peace within you as you rest! Gray-eyed dawn smiles 'hello' to the somber departing night, checkering the eastern clouds with streaks of morning light – I'll stop at the holy Father's monastery cell, to seek his help and my good fortune tell…."

——— ♥ ———

Friar Laurence works quietly away in the garden of the ancient monastery.

"Now before the sun opens his burning eye, to greet the day and the dank night dew to dry, I must fill up this willow basket of ours, with deadly herbs and rare-nectar flowers. The good earth, which acts as Nature's tomb," he observes thoughtfully, "is the very same place which serves as its womb – the place where all plants and flowers and growing things take nourishment from their earthly mother's bosom. And while it is true many of them have wholesome healing properties, there are those that have none at all. They are so very very different – great the benefits of so many plants, herbs and minerals, whose qualities – no matter how bad – can be exceptionally helpful, and yet there are those which although good, if used in ways they're not meant to be can do serious harm. Virtue itself can become a vice if misapplied, and vice in certain situations, is justified."

Romeo enters the garden, unseen by Friar Laurence, who brings a flower he has just picked up to his face for a closer look.

"Within the tender seeds of this weak flower, a poison exists of incredible power: if you sniff it, the scent is divine; while if you taste it, your heart stops beating in a few seconds' time. Two such potent opposites present in one place, as true in plants as in the human race – grace and rude will. And where the latter is predominant, death eventually consumes the person, or eats up the plant."

"Good morning, Father." Romeo has walked up behind Friar Laurence.

"Bless you, son. What bird roused you so early from that bed of yours? I wonder if there's something going on in that head of yours? Worries keep watch in every old man's eye, and where there is worry, sleep will never lie. But the innocent youth, with little on his mind, takes to his bed and sleeps a long time. This earliness suggests an illness is in sight. Or if not that, I hit it right in thinking our Romeo has not been to bed tonight."

"The last part is true; I had something better than sleep," Romeo informs him.

"May the Lord forgive you, were you with Rosaline?"

"With Rosaline? Good holy Father, no!"

"Well, I'm glad to hear that."

"I have forgotten that name. It brought me nothing but trouble."

"So where have you been then?"

"Feasting with my enemy. And one of them wounded me, at the

same time as I inflicted a wound myself," Romeo declares. "The only hope for both of us, Father, lies in medicine provided by you; I harbor no hatred over this, for I appeal on behalf of my opponent too."

"Let's get to the point, young man. A confession full of riddles will get you a pardon full of them as well."

"All right. I should tell you then, I have my heart set on the fair daughter of rich Capulet. Hers is set on mine as well, so we would like to get married. When, where and how we met and made this our decision, right now I can't really say. But this I devoutly pray: that you consent to marry us today."

"My goodness, Romeo! What a change has taken place! Is Rosaline, whom you were completely enamored with, to be given up so readily? Perhaps it's true a young man's love is more in his eyes than in his heart. Goodness gracious, when I think how many tears were shed over Rosaline, how much good water was wasted making that love grow. I can still hear your groans and sighs ringing in my ears: your face is still covered with the stains of those old tears. Given that you were being yourself and your anguish over Rosaline was sincere, this represents a considerable change. Heed my words, though: women can prove unfaithful if their men are that way too."

"But you scolded me so often for loving Rosaline."

"For being infatuated with her," Friar Laurence clarifies, "not for loving her, my boy."

"You told me to bury my love."

"But not in one grave just so you can start digging another."

"Please don't scold me this time – the one I love now returns my feelings and offers hers to me in a way that Rosaline never did."

"Perhaps because she knew you loved by the book when you hadn't yet learned to read, so to speak. But come along my fickle young friend. In one respect I think I can be of help. For such an alliance may work out for the best, if it puts your families' rancor to rest."

"Let's hurry, then. There's not much time."

"Wisely and slow," Friar Laurence cautions, "they stumble that run too fast."

——— ♥ ———

Several hours later, Benvolio and Mercutio are taking a morning stroll along the street.

"Where the devil can Romeo be?" Mercutio demands. "Didn't he go home at all last night?"

"Apparently not, according to his father," Benvolio says, yawning.

"That cold-hearted tease Rosaline is driving him crazy."

"As it turns out, old Capulet's kinsman Tybalt has sent a letter to Romeo's father."

"A challenge, I bet."

"Romeo will answer it."

"Any self-respecting man would."

"I don't think he has any choice. He'll fight fire with fire."

"Unfortunately for Romeo, he's already been burned. Seared with a woman's flaming beauty, his mind clouded with the smoke of too many love songs, the core of his heart split in two with the red-hot shaft of Cupid's arrow. Will he be able to take on Tybalt?"

"Why, what's so special about Tybalt?"

"Besides his reputation as 'the prince of cats' he's also considered one of the best swordsmen around. He could have written a book on fighting the perfect duel – slice off the top button of your shirt in the blink of an eye. He has the rules for taking offence and making accusations down pat. But more than anything else, he's got the moves of an expert." Drawing his sword, he uses it to demonstrate. "The lunging attack, the defensive back hand, the lethal *hai!*

"The what?"

"The *hai!* The thrust!" he declares with an elaborate flourish. "Used by these lisping, affected types who like tossing around foreign words to impress people. 'Oh indeed, he's *merveilleux avec le sabre. Un homme tres courageux. Une putain adroite!*" he scoffs. It's pathetic how we're surrounded by these no-talent poseurs who know all the fashionable terms but nothing about the art of sword fighting. *Bon* this, *bon* that!"

"There's Romeo!" Benvolio cries. "There's Romeo!"

"Oh – Me, without the Ro – looks like he's wasting away. Flesh, flesh, what's happening here?" Mercutio inquires, swishing his sword past Romeo's cheeks, arms and sides. "Signor Romeo, *bon jour.* There's a French 'good morning' to go with your loose French garb." With the point of his sword he flips the white cloth of Romeo's shirt, which is undone and hanging open. "You duped us pretty well last night."

"Good morning to both of you. What do you mean I 'duped' you?"

"The slip, man. You gave us the slip. Don't play dumb."

"My apologies. It was important, that's all. The situation I was in. I had to forego the usual courtesies."

"In other words you couldn't spare a moment just to bend over?" Mercutio quips.

"No time for curtsies," Romeo replies, playing along.

"Exactly."

"A courteous explanation."

"Ahhh, I'm your man when it comes to courtesy."

"Witty too."

"Very."

"Are you saying I'm not?" Romeo demands as if offended.

"Let's just see. Take your shoes, for instance. If you wear them out, does that mean the sole is worn, or the soul has worn them out and about?"

"A worn out sole, I should warn you, is not well worn by a soul like me."

"Quick, Benvolio," Mercutio protests in mock peril, "catch me before I lose this battle of the wits."

Grabbing Mercutio's sword as he pretends to swoon, Romeo jabs the air around a playfully reeling Mercutio.

"Come on, keep it up or I'll be the winner," Romeo teases.

"A wild goose chase like this – you'll completely outwit me. You have more wild goose in just one of your wits than I have in all five of mine."

"Ah, but you've always been the goose I love to gander at."

"I'll bite your ear for a comment like that."

"Oh no, sweet goose, please spare me!"

"I have to say, your wit is tart and saucy."

"Best served by a saucy tart, I'm sure."

"Isn't this better than moaning and groaning about love?" Mercutio chuckles. "You're back to being Romeo. You're your old self again. Admit it, this whole love business just turns us into great drooling idiots walking around with our tongues hanging out till we find a hole to hide our you-know-what in –"

"Hold on, hold on," Benvolio warns.

"Don't make me stop," Mercutio protests, "I'm just getting to the best part."

"The dirty part, you mean."

"Benvolio, come on. That's not fair. I was going to keep it short and sweet for a change –"

"There's short and sweet for you," Romeo remarks as Nurse in a broad, billowing dress bustles boldly past the three young men with a Capulet family escort, a meek, none-too-bright fellow whose name is Peter.

"A sail!" Romeo calls. "A sail!"

"Assail it is!" Mercutio joins in. "Ahoy, ahoy! A skirt and her boy!" He darts over and makes rude gestures behind Nurse's back. Romeo and Benvolio are meanwhile having fun with the dim-witted Peter.

"Peter!" Nurse demands, trying to move past the young men.

"Just a minute, m'am."

"Give me my fan."

"Yes Peter," Mercutio jokes. "She wants to hide her face because the fan is so much better for us to look at."

"Good morning, gentlemen," Nurse says stiffly.

"Good evening, fair gentlewoman," Mercutio snickers.

"Good evening?"

"Oh yes, for the eager hand of the dial is now upon the prick of noon."

"Get away with you!" Nurse responds, disgusted. "What kind of man are you?"

"One, gentlewoman, who has been made to ruin himself," Romeo informs her.

"I can see that, sir. 'Made to ruin himself.' That's it, sir. But gentlemen, can any of you tell me where I might find the young Romeo?"

"I can," says Romeo. "But young Romeo might appear older when you find him, than he was when you asked for him. I am the youngest one who goes by that name, for better or worse."

"You speak so well, sir."

"Better than one who's worse," Mercutio winks. "And so wise, so wise...."

Nurse presses on. "If you are he," she declares, "I need to have a word with you in conference."

"She will *indite* him home for supper, next," Benvolio laughs, making fun of her pronunciation.

"I knew it, she's a randy old rabbit!" Mercutio cries. "A randy one! Randy, I tell you!" He lifts the corner of her dress and peeks under – "Ah hah!! – until Nurse bats him away with her fan.

"What was that?" Romeo grins.

As Mercutio strolls off across the square he begins singing a lewd song.

"*A hoary old hare, yes a hoary old hare, with plenty of spring in her hop. But a hare that is hoary, will never find glory, until she can learn to say 'Stop!'* Romeo, will you be going to your father's for lunch?"

"Yes, I'll meet you there," he says.

Now that the others are gone, a badly flustered Nurse takes a moment to recover from the unsettling encounter.

"If you don't mind my asking, sir, who was that rude rascal so full of saucy remarks?"

"A gentleman who loves to hear himself talk. He can come out with more in a minute than most people can think of saying in a month."

"Well, if he ever comes near me again I'll take care of him. I'm strong enough to handle him and twenty other louts like him if I need to. If not, I can find people who will. The worthless scoundrel. I'm not one of his chippies – I'm no floozy!"

She turns angrily on her escort, Peter.

"And you! Just standing there, letting the man make advances."

"I didn't see the man making advances," Peter says simply. "If I had, I would have taken out my weapon right away. I promise you, I can draw my sword as fast as any other man if there's the opportunity for a good quarrel, and if the law's on my side."

"I'm so upset right now my whole body's shaking," Nurse declares. "The ill- mannered boor! But, I would like a word with you, sir, if I could. As I told you, the young woman I work for sent me to find you. What she wanted me to say, I'll save for last. First I want you to know that if your plan is to lead her down the garden path, as they say, that would be a vile thing to do. She's still young, and if you should mislead her in any way it would be a conniving thing to do to a gentlewoman like her, a cowardly, conniving thing, as I said."

"Nurse, my compliments to your lady, but I have to say – "

"Dear man, I will tell her exactly that, then. She'll be overjoyed."

"You'll tell her what?" Romeo asks perplexed. "You haven't heard what I was going to say."

"I will tell her, sir, that you have to say – which, it seems to me, is a gentlemanlike offer."

Ignoring her confusion, Romeo pulls Nurse aside. "Have her arrange to be at Friar Laurence's for confession this afternoon. We will make our confession and then be married. Here's something for your help."

"Oh no, sir. I couldn't take a penny."

"I insist." He presses the money on her.

"This afternoon, sir? Well, she will be there."

"And also, good Nurse, within the hour a man will meet you behind the abbey wall and give you the rope ladder I'll use to reach my joy in her room tonight. Farewell, be trustworthy and I'll see that you're rewarded for your efforts. Farewell. Give my love to your mistress."

"Good heavens, just a minute, sir!"

"What's the matter?"

"Is your man reliable? You know what they say: loose lips, sink ships."

"I promise you, my man's as solid as they come."

"Well, I only mention it since my mistress is such a sweet young girl. Goodness me," Nurse babbles, "when she was a little chattering thing – oh I should tell you, there is a nobleman here in town named Paris, who would like to have a share of the goods too, if you know what I mean, but she, sweet girl, would just as soon kiss a toad as kiss him. I make her angry at times because I tell her Paris is the perfect catch, but I have to admit, when I say so she just goes white as a sheet. Don't rosemary and Romeo begin with the same letter?"

"Of course. Both with an *R*. What of that?"

"Silly man! That's how a dog growls: *Rrrrrr*. No, that begins with another letter, you're right. *Are*…but it seemed that sounded the nicest, you and rosemary, so I thought you'd like – "

"I would like you to give my love to your lady," Romeo tells her and rushes away.

"Of course! A thousand times!" Nurse calls after him. "Peter!"

"Hang on," the simple fellow says, busy gawking at something.

"No, right now!"

♥

Juliet is pacing anxiously in the front courtyard of the Capulet house.

"I sent her out at nine o'clock and she promised to be back in half an hour. Perhaps she couldn't find him. No, that can't be. Oh! She is so inept sometimes. Love's messengers should move at the speed of light, the way sunbeams make shadows vanish on the hillside. The day's half over. I've been waiting three whole hours and she's still not back. If she had the feelings and the urges in her blood that I do, she'd move so much faster getting word to my love and returning with his message to me. But old people act as if they're nearly dead – heavy, slow, lethargic and dull as lead."

Yet no sooner has she finished denouncing Nurse in frustration than she sees her and Peter entering the courtyard.

"Oh, thank God she's back!" Juliet rejoices and runs to meet them. "Sweet Nurse, what news? Did you meet with him? Send your man away and tell me."

"Peter, stay at the gate," Nurse orders.

Juliet notices a forlorn expression on Nurse's face. "Good woman, why are you looking so sad? If the news isn't good, at least tell it to me as pleasantly as you can. And if it is good, you should be ashamed of yourself for playing with me by wearing such a sorry face."

"I'm so tired," Nurse sighs wearily. "Give me a moment. Lord, how my bones are aching – what an ordeal I've had!"

"I wish you had my bones and I your news. Come Nurse, please please tell me."

"What's the big hurry? Can't you be patient, seeing that I'm all out of breath?"

"How can you be out of breath when you've got plenty enough to complain about being all out of breath? The excuse you make for delaying is taking up more time than the news you're making excuses for not telling me. Is it good or bad? Let me know and either way I'll accept the fact. But for goodness sake, just tell me: is it good or is it bad?"

"Well, you've made a foolish choice. You don't know how to choose a man. Romeo? No, definitely not. Though he's better looking than most men, and though his body's nothing to sneeze at, still, I'd say he compares quite favorably to most other men. He's not exactly tops in courtesy, yet I can vouch for the fact he's gentle as a lamb. Run along now. You'll have to let God take care of it. Have you had your lunch yet?"

"No, no. But I knew most of this before. What did he say about getting married? What about that?"

"Lord, what a headache! It's throbbing like it'll shatter in twenty pieces any minute now. My back too –oh, my back! Curse you for sending me out to catch my death traipsing all over town."

"Look, I'm sorry you're not feeling well. But sweet, sweet, sweet Nurse," Juliet pleads in exasperation, "tell me what my love said!"

"Your love says, like an honest gentleman, and a courteous, and a kind, and a handsome, and I imagine a virtuous one too – where's your mother?"

"My mother? She's in the house where she should be. This sounds very peculiar. 'Your love says, like an honest gentleman, "Where's your mother?"'"

"Good God, dear girl, why are you so angry? Is this the thanks I get? From now on you can do your messages yourself."

At her wit's end, Juliet puts her foot down. "Stop making such a terrible fuss. Just tell me what Romeo said. Now."

"Do you have permission to go to confession today?"

"I do."

"Then get yourself over to Friar Laurence's cell," Nurse says. "A husband is waiting there to make you his wife! Look at you blush – well, it is the kind of news to turn a girl's face red. Off to the church with you. I'll go and fetch the ladder by which your lover will climb to join you in the bird's nest after dark," she explains with a smirking grin. "The burdens I have to bear in the name of pleasure – though you'll be the one bearing the burden tonight, my girl. On your way! I'm off to lunch. Hurry over to the chapel."

"I'll hurry to happy fortune. Dearest Nurse, farewell."

———— ♥ ————

Friar Laurence and Romeo walk along a corridor toward the chapel where the wedding ceremony will take place.

"May heaven look favorably upon this holy act, so that afterwards we shall have nothing to be sorry about," Friar Laurence says.

"Amen, amen, but even if there is something to be sorry for, it will never equal the joy I experience every minute we're together. Once you have joined our hands in marriage, love-devouring death can do whatever it pleases: it's enough for me that I can call her mine."

"Extreme pleasures ultimately produce extreme results," Friar Laurence cautions, "their intensity destroying the very thing which is created – like fire and gunpowder, which explode the instant they meet. Bear in mind too, that the sweetest honey is repulsive in its own deliciousness, the taste destroying honey's own appetite for sweetness. Therefore love in moderation; long lasting love does so. 'Too quick' can be as damaging as 'too slow."

He has barely finished speaking when Juliet appears, rushing in her simple white dress and slippered feet to embrace Romeo.

"Here is the bride herself, so nimble and light on her feet she could dance across spiders' webs in the still, summer air without disturbing them."

"Good evening, holy Father."

"Romeo and I are grateful you've come, my dear."

"He couldn't be more grateful than I am to be here."

The young lovers gaze longingly at one another.

"Oh Juliet, if your joy is as great as mine, and you are able to put it into words, then I wish you would because I am unable to express the unimaginable happiness in store for us on this occasion."

"My imagination is overflowing with humble gratitude. Those who can calculate their wealth are poor compared with me: whose true love has grown so vast I can't begin to estimate even half the worth your love has brought me."

"Come along with me then," Friar Laurence says solemnly, "and we will promptly attend to the matter at hand, for with due respect you can't enjoy each other alone, till holy church incorporate the two as one."

Mercutio, Benvolio and a group of Montague men are strolling idly through the public square as the afternoon sun beats down.

"Listen, Mercutio, why don't we just go home. It's blazing hot, the Capulets are in the vicinity, and if we meet them there's bound to be a fight."

"Benvolio, you're like one of those fellows who, when he goes into a tavern, slaps his sword down on the table with a flourish and declares 'I pray to God I don't have to use this sword today', and by the time you're on your second pint, you're tapping the tapster with the tip of your sword in hopes of stirring something up."

"You really think I'm like that?"

"Come on, you're as hot-tempered as any man in Italy when you're in a bad mood – as easily provoked to anger as you are angry to be provoked."

"And what of it?"

"Well, if there were two of you, you wouldn't be around very long, for one of you would kill the other. You? Why, you'd quarrel with a man who has a hair more or a hair less in his beard than you; you'd quarrel with a man for cracking nuts simply because you have hazel eyes. Who but you can spot a quarrel from a mile away? Your head is as full of quarrels as an egg is full of yolk, even though that same head has been beaten in quarrel after quarrel. Remember when you tangled with a man coughing in the street, because he woke up a dog that was sleeping? And wasn't it you who trounced a tailor for wearing his new holiday clothes before the holidays began? And another fellow for tying his shoes with broken laces? And yet you want to lecture *me* about quarreling!"

"If I were as fond of quarreling as you are," Benvolio argues in his own defence, "nobody would bet on me to live into my twenties."

"Into your twenties!" Mercutio laughs. "Your twenties!" Facing Benvolio, he doesn't see that behind him Tybalt, Petruchio and a band of Capulet men have come into view.

"Wouldn't you know it," Benvolio says uneasily, "here come some of the Capulets."

"Who cares," Mercutio shrugs.

Tybalt leads the way. "Stay back while I talk to them," he orders his followers. "Good afternoon, gentlemen. A word with one of you."

"Just a word?" Mercutio says. "Why not throw something else in, like maybe a blow?"

"I'm all for that," Tybalt replies testily, "if you give me a good reason."

"Who needs a reason?"

"Mercutio, you consort with Romeo."

"Consort?" Mercutio scoffs. "What, do you take us for a bunch of musicians? If you want to make musicians out of us, be ready to hear plenty of discords. Beginning with this. Here's my baton, it might make you dance! God damn you, consort!"

Benvolio restrains him so he can't draw his sword. "We're standing in a public place," he warns, "surrounded by all kinds of people. It's better if we go somewhere private and take a look at the situation, or else just head on our way. We're in full view right now. Everyone can see us."

"People's eyes were made for looking. Let them look. I'm not backing down for any man, much less a Capulet."

Tybalt, however, has noticed Romeo approaching in the square.

"Never mind, sir. Here comes the lackey follower I'm looking for."

"Funny he doesn't seem to be wearing servant's clothes like you are, Tybalt. Maybe you should go on ahead to the dueling field. He can walk behind you, which in that sense would make him the lackey follower."

Ignoring the slight, Tybalt is intent on talking to Romeo.

"What I feel toward you, Romeo, prevents me from addressing you as anything but a measly scoundrel."

"Tybalt, there's a reason for me to consider you a friend now. There's no need for such hostility: I'm no scoundrel, measly or otherwise, so farewell. You've got the wrong man."

"Not at all. There's no excuse for the offensive way you dealt with me last night. Turn and draw."

"What are you talking about? I did nothing to offend you. In fact, I regard you more highly than you can imagine, even though you don't know the reason why, at this point. So, good Capulet – a name I now value as much as my own – don't insult me."

Mercutio can hardly restrain himself. "Of all the weak and shameful surrenders – *alla stoc-cat-a* is the honorable way!" He takes out his sword and brandishes it, but Tybalt doesn't touch his. "You rat-catcher, are you backing down then?"

"What do you want with me?"

"Just one of your nine lives, good King of Cats, which I will take right now, and then thrash the other eight to pieces when I'm done. Won't you grab your weapon in case mine makes mincemeat of you before you get it out?"

"The pleasure would be mine," Tybalt says, drawing his sword.

"Dear Mercutio, put it away," Romeo urges.

"Come sir, let's see what you can do!"

And the fight begins in earnest, the two men going at each other in a clash of rattling swords.

"Draw Benvolio and force them to put their weapons down!" Romeo shouts.

"Gentlemen, for pity's sake, stop this violence. Tybalt! Mercutio! The Prince has outlawed fighting! Quit, Tybalt! Dear Mercutio!"

In a desperate move, Romeo steps between the two swordsmen and tries to part them. Ever alert, Tybalt catches Mercutio unawares and thrusts his sword under Romeo's arm, plunging the blade into his opponent's chest.

"Run for it, Tybalt!" a Capulet follower yells when he sees Mercutio collapsing in Romeo's arms.

"I am wounded," Mercutio speaks through his pain. "A curse on both your houses. I'm wounded. Is he gone, and not a mark on him?"

"What, have you really been hurt?" Benvolio cries in disbelief.

"Yes yes, a scratch, a scratch. Although it's enough. Where is my lad? Go boy," he orders his young attendant, "fetch me a surgeon."

"Courage, my friend, the wound can't be too serious," Romeo says.

"Not as deep as a well, nor wide as a church door. But it is enough, it will do the trick. Ask for me tomorrow and you will find me a grave man," Mercutio kids light-heartedly, his energy draining away rapidly. "I'm not long for this world. A curse on both your houses, I say. It's disgusting – a dog, a rat, a mouse, a cat, they should be the ones to scratch a man to death. Yet here am I, a braggart, a rogue, a villain, who fights by all the rules – why on earth did you come between us Romeo? He stabbed me underneath your arm."

Still reeling with the shock of such a tragic event, Romeo meets Mercutio's half-closed eyes. "I thought it was for the best"

"Help me into someone's house, Benvolio, before I fall unconscious. A curse on both your houses," he rails, barely audible now. "They have made worm food of me. I'm done for, and soon. Your houses!"

Benvolio carries his dying friend off. Romeo remains behind, brooding on what has just happened.

"This good man is dying because of me," he says. "This relative of the Prince, this true friend, and our good name disgraced by Tybalt's treachery – Tybalt who an hour ago became my cousin. Oh sweet Juliet, I fear your beauty might have weakened me, might have softened the steely spirit of my courage."

"Oh Romeo, Romeo," Benvolio cries helplessly, "brave Mercutio is dead, that gallant soul of his risen to the clouds, now that it has parted from the earth."

"This day's dark deed in future days will loom; this act of mine invokes a dire, woeful gloom," Romeo murmurs gravely.

"Tybalt is coming back," Benvolio announces, "and he's more furious than ever."

"Back to gloat in triumph that Mercutio is slain," Romeo says scornfully. "So much for tolerance and respect, hot-blooded fury guide my conduct now! Tybalt, take back the 'villain' you called me less than an hour ago, for Mercutio's only a little way above our heads, waiting for you to keep him company. Either you or I, or both of us, must be prepared to join him."

"You pathetic child, who consorted with him here, shall soon be with him there."

"We will see!" Romeo declares in fierce defiance.

Swords drawn, they fight ruthlessly until Tybalt falls, killed instantly by a deep thrust from Romeo's sword.

"Be gone, Romeo," Benvolio advises, "citizens are taking up arms now that Tybalt has been slain too. Don't just stand there. The Prince will condemn you to death once you're captured. Flee, run away!"

"How could I have become fortune's fool…"

"What are you waiting for?" Benvolio demands as he hurries Romeo on his way.

"Which way did the man go who killed Mercutio?" a citizen wants to know. "Tybalt the murderer, which way did he run?"

"There lies Tybalt."

"Come sir," one citizen calls to another, "go with me to find the killer. I command you in the Prince's name to obey!"

In a short while the tumult has spread through the streets, only the sudden appearance of the Prince restoring order. He glares at Montague and Capulet, their wives and followers, and demands an explanation.

"Where are the dastardly culprits who created this havoc?" he storms.

"Most noble Prince," Benvolio says stepping forward, "I can explain how things unfolded and tell you how a harmless situation grew out of control. Tybalt lies dead just over there, slain by young Romeo, who killed him because he took the life of your kinsman, Mercutio."

"Tybalt, my nephew, my brother's child?" Lady Capulet gasps. "My honored Prince," she continues, then turns, grief-stricken, to Capulet, "my loving husband…" Struggling to keep her composure, Lady Capulet turns back to the Prince. "The blood of my dear relative has been spilled needlessly. As you wield authority, your Honor, I urge that the blood of a Montague be shed in return for the shedding of ours. Oh nephew, nephew," she mourns.

The Prince confronts Benvolio.

"Who started the fight?" he asks firmly.

"Tybalt did. Romeo spoke courteously about how foolish the animosity between the two families had become, and he reminded Tybalt how you yourself had outlawed it. He was very calm, peaceful and polite in the way he talked, yet it fell on deaf ears. Tybalt was so enraged he drew his sword and went at Mercutio savagely. As angry as Tybalt, he had no choice but to defend himself, both men exchanging blows with deadly dexterity until Romeo jumped between them and shouted for them to stop, waving his arms in their faces so they would lower their swords. However, Tybalt saw an opportunity and lunged at Mercutio from behind, killing him almost instantly.

"Naturally Tybalt fled from the scene of his crime, however in a few moments remorseful Romeo decided it was his duty to go after the murderer and avenge Mercutio's death. They confronted each other at close quarters and went at it so fast and furiously there was nothing any of us could do to stop them. Before we knew it, it was too late. With Tybalt slain, Romeo had no choice but to turn and fly. This is the truth, or let Benvolio die."

"Lies! He is a kinsman to the Montague, for heaven's sake!" Lady Capulet protests. "You can't expect him to tell us the truth. There must have been two-dozen people involved in this horrible melee – how could only one of them lose his life? No, Prince. In the name of justice I demand that as Romeo killed Tybalt, Romeo must now die."

"Romeo killed Tybalt, but he killed Mercutio. Is taking yet another life the price to be paid for this?"

"Not Romeo's, Prince," Montague pleads. "He was Mercutio's friend. His offence was taking it upon himself to do what our law calls for: the life of Tybalt."

"And for that offence he is exiled from Verona as of this moment. I have grief of my own to contend with here: my blood lies bleeding too as a result of your despicable feuding. But I am imposing such an enormous fine that you will all be sorry for the loss you have caused me to suffer. I will turn a deaf ear to pleading and excuses; neither tears nor entreaties will lead me to overlook these abuses. Therefore make none. Let Romeo leave Verona immediately. Remove Tybalt's body and await my further will. Mercy doesn't prevent murder; it only pardons those who kill."

—— ♥ ——

In her bedroom, Juliet waits restlessly for her husband Romeo.

"Speed toward the end of day you horses galloping the sun's chariot across the sky, so that the moon can shine and love-inducing night draw its cloudy curtains around me to greet Romeo as he leaps noiselessly and unseen into my waiting arms. In light from their own beauty, lovers can see through darkness to perform their amorous rites, or if love is truly blind, that is most suitable of all. Come, stately night, dressed in deepest black, teach me how to lose a game in which the stakes are two pristine young virgins. But hide my blushing maiden face in the folds of your long black cloak, till one unpracticed in the ways of love grows bold and learns the acts of true love's simple modesty.

"Come night, come Romeo, come you day into night, where you will lie upon the wings of night whiter than new snow upon a raven's back. Come gentle night, come loving black-browed night – give me my Romeo so that when I die you shall take him and cut him out in little stars, and he will make the face of heaven so fine that all the world will be in love with night, and cease worshipping the garish sun. Oh, I have purchased the mansion of true love but not yet possessed it, and like that house, I have been sold, though my rooms have yet to be enjoyed.

"How tediously long this day seems, like the night before a thrilling event for the impatient child who has all new clothes, but must wait to try them on. Why, here is Nurse now. I know she brings word – just hearing her speak Romeo's name will be joyous. What news Nurse? What do you have there? The ropes that Romeo wanted?

"Yes yes, the ropes," Nurse says sharply.

"So, what news have you brought me? But why are you wringing your hands like that?"

"It's horrible – he's dead, he's dead, he's dead! We are ruined, lady, ruined! It's horrible, he's gone, he's killed, he's dead!"

"Can heaven be so jealous?"

"Heaven can't be, but Romeo can. Oh Romeo, Romeo! Who would have thought it possible, Romeo?"

"You're a devil to torment me this way – did Romeo kill himself? Tell me 'Aye' and that simple vowel 'I' will rid the serpent murder of its deadly sting. I am not I if there is such an 'Aye.' If he has been slain please say 'Aye' or if not, 'No'; the briefest sound will give me comfort or seize me with sorrow."

"I saw the wound," Nurse says, choking back tears, "saw it with my own eyes – God save me – here on his manly chest." She crosses her heart. "A pitiful looking corpse, bloody and pitiful. Pale, pale as ashes he was, smeared in blood with gory blood-rimmed wounds – I fainted at the sight."

"Oh break my poor heart, my poor heart break at once! Lock my eyes away in prison, never to look upon freedom ever again. Ready my lifeless body for its return to the earth – bear my sorrow-filled coffin to the grave."

"Oh Tybalt, Tybalt, the best friend I had," Nurse wails in sorrow. "Oh courteous Tybalt, you delightful man. I never thought I'd live to see you dead."

Juliet freezes, stunned by what Nurse has just said.

"What storm is this now blowing from a different direction? Is Romeo slaughtered and Tybalt dead as well? My dearest cousin and my beloved husband? Then sound the dreadful trumpet for general doom. For what is there left to live for if these two are gone?"

"Tybalt is gone, but Romeo is banished," Nurse says, "banished for killing Tybalt."

"No! Did Romeo's hand shed Tybalt's blood?"

"It did, it did, most awfully, it did."

It takes a moment for Juliet to let this news sink in. "Oh serpent heart hidden with a flowering face. Did a dragon ever live in such a fine lair? Beautiful tyrant, angelic fiend, dove-feathered raven, wolf-ravenous lamb! Despised substance, masked with such seeming goodness! The opposite of everything you seemed to be! What did nature do in hell to disguise the spirit of something so foul, as a man so fair? Was a book containing such terrible matter ever so finely bound? Oh, that deception could dwell in such a regal palace."

"You can't trust men," Nurse declares, "you can't have faith in them, can't expect them to be honest. They lie, break their promises, they're all hypocrites, I say. Where's the servant boy? Bring me a glass of spirits!" she calls. "All this grief, these woes, these sorrows, they're making me old before my time. Shame on Romeo!"

"Your tongue should receive a scalding for saying such a thing! He was not born to be talked about like that. Shame is ashamed to be seen on his face, for he has the quality of honor which would see him crowned sole monarch in any kingdom in the world. Oh how selfish I was to be so critical of him myself."

"How can you speak well of the man that killed your cousin?" Nurse demands.

"How can I speak badly of the man who is my husband? The unfortunate man, who will redeem his name when I, his wife of three hours, have so maligned it? Though I need to know why he killed my cousin – that same cousin who would have killed my husband. Back, foolish tears, back to the spring from which you came, your welling drops flow from sorrow, yet strangely you offer yourselves in the name of joy as well. My husband lives, who Tybalt would have killed, and Tybalt's dead, who would have killed my husband. This is cause for happiness, so why am I on the verge of weeping?

"But there was a word, one worse than Tybalt – 'dead', that murdered other thoughts. If only it had not been said, but it presses into my memory like a guilty deed does in a sinner's mind. Tybalt – dead. But Romeo – banished. That 'banished', that one word 'banished' has erased ten thousand 'Tybalts': his death was sorrow enough, if it had ended there. Yet if sorrow is accompanied by other griefs, why then, when she said 'Tybalt's dead', didn't I think of his father or mother, or both, which custom calls for?

"Instead, when I learned how he had died, my only thought was 'Romeo is banished': which was like saying father, mother, Tybalt, Romeo and Juliet were slain as well, all dead. Romeo is banished. There is no end to what that means for me – no limit, scope or boundary to what dies with those words. And there are none which can sound my sorrow."

In shock and grief, Juliet can only stare at her hands.

"Where are my father and mother?" she asks quietly.

"Weeping and wailing over Tybalt's body. I can take you to them if you wish."

"Are they washing his wounds with their tears? When theirs are dry for him, mine will all have been shed for Romeo's banishment. Take this rope ladder away. Poor ropes, you have been tricked, both you and I, for Romeo is exiled. You were the path that would have led him to my bed, but I, a maid, will die a widow-maid instead. Come, cords, come Nurse. I shall go to my wedding bed, and death, not Romeo, take my virgin maidenhead."

"You lie down, then," Nurse tells Juliet in an effort to console her. "I'll find Romeo and bring him to comfort you. I think I know where he might be. Listen to me now: your Romeo will be here with you tonight. I'll go to him. He's hiding at Laurence's cell."

"Oh find him, give this ring to my one true knight, and ask him here to take his last farewell."

—— ♥ ——

Friar Laurence hastens along a corridor in his residence searching for Romeo. "Where are you Romeo, you fearful man? You can come out now, though I have to say trouble seems to love everything about you, as if you were wedded to calamity."

Romeo slips out of his hiding place and approaches Friar Laurence.

"What is the news, Father? What is the Prince's verdict? What further will come my way?"

"You've grown too attached to your distress, my dear boy."

"How close is doomsday to the Prince's doom?"

"He issued a gentler judgment than you might have expected: banishment instead of death."

"Banishment? Be kind and say it was 'death', for the prospect of exile is more terrifying. Please say it wasn't banishment."

"Banished from Verona for life. But don't despair, for the world is broad and wide, full of many possibilities."

"Not for me," Romeo replies grimly. "For me there is no world beyond Verona. 'Banished' is banished from the world, and exiled from this world is death. Death is preferable to 'banished'. Calling death 'banished' is like cutting off my head with a sharp, gold axe and then smiling that at least the job was done with one good stroke."

"Don't be so ungrateful. Murder is a deadly sin, Romeo, a crime punishable by execution. The prince has kindly taken your part by setting aside the law and substituting banishment for death. He's being merciful, even if you don't see it that way."

"It's torture, Father, not mercy. Life is being here with Juliet, don't you see? Every cat and dog and little mouse can look upon her, but Romeo cannot. The lowliest creatures have more dignity, worth and opportunity to love than I. They may seize on the white wonder of her hand and steal immortal blessing from her lips – lips which continue to blush in pure, virgin innocence, where even the thought of a kiss remains sinful. But Romeo cannot, because he is banished. Other men continue to be free, but I am forced to go away. You say exile is not death? Haven't you a poison you could mix? Some razor-sharp knife I could use? Some means of a quick death that would kill me more humanely than 'banished'? The damned in hell refer to themselves using that word, Father. How can you have the heart, being a man of God, confession and forgiveness – and supposedly my friend – to abuse me with that word 'banished'?"

"Listen to me you crazy fool – "

"Are you going to extol banishment some more?"

"No, I only want to help you cope with it by sharing some aspects of philosophy people often turn to in times of adversity."

"But 'banished'. What does philosophy have to do with it? Unless it can somehow create another Juliet, transplant a whole town to another place, and reverse a Prince's verdict – it won't help, it won't solve anything. So please don't talk to me about philosophy."

"I see madmen have no ears."

"How can they when wise men have no eyes?"

"Let me at least discuss the situation."

"You can't talk about what you don't feel. If you were as young as

I, Juliet your new wife, Tybalt murdered, your mind distraught, and you were banished like I am, then you could talk to me – then you could tear out your hair and fall upon the ground as I do now to take measurements for my grave – "

Overwhelmed, he slumps to the floor in tears, at the same moment as a loud knock comes at Friar Laurence's door.

"Someone's here, get up! Go and hide until I see who it is."

"No. I'll let the sound of my suffering shroud me in invisible mist so I simply vanish."

The person knocks on the door again.

"Listen to that – who's there? – get up, Romeo, you'll be taken away – just a minute! – stand up, son."

The knocking continues, growing louder.

"Go to my study – I'm coming! – for goodness sake, what nonsense is this – I'm coming, I'm coming!"

The rapping on the door has become extremely insistent.

"Who knocks so hard? Where are you from? What do you want?"

"Let me in and I'll tell you," says Nurse from the other side of the door. "I come from Lady Juliet."

"Come in then."

The Nurse rushes in and clutches the brown cloth of Friar Laurence's robe.

"Oh holy Friar, you must tell me where Romeo is," she says, in high anxiety.

"There on the ground," Friar Laurence points, "drunk on his own tears."

"He's in the same condition as my mistress. What a sad situation, what a sorry predicament. She's doing the same thing, weeping and blubbering, blubbering and weeping."

The Nurse walks over to Romeo and bends down.

"Get on your feet, young man," she tells him sternly. "Stand up like a man, for Juliet's sake. Come now, get to your feet for her sake. What's got into you?

Romeo gets to his feet slowly, not recognizing her at first.

"Nurse," he mutters, regaining his composure.

"Yes sir, yes sir, death puts an end to everything."

"What was it you said about Juliet? How is she? Does she take me for an out-and-out murderer, now that I have stained our newfound joy with the blood of a dear relative? Where is she now? How is she doing? What does my secret wife have to say concerning our fractured love?"

"She says nothing, sir. Just weeps and weeps for all she's worth, falls on her bed and starts up again, calling for Tybalt, crying out your name, and then she buries her head in the pillow and sobs uncontrollably."

"Like the name Romeo had been shot from a gun leveled at her heart, murdering her with the name that owns the hands that murdered her kinsman!" Romeo shrieks in despair as he draws his dagger, "Tell me, Friar, please just tell me, in what vile part of this anatomy has my name come to live? Tell me, so I can ransack the hateful mansion!"

"Put the dagger down!" Friar Laurence commands, grabbing Romeo by the wrist and wrestling the weapon away from him. "Do you call yourself a man? In appearance you certainly are, but your tears are womanish, your frantic actions the instinctive wrath of a wild animal. You're a whimpering woman masquerading as a man, and a poor performer on both counts. You amaze me. By my holy vows, I took you for someone with a much better temperament than this. You killed Tybalt. Now you want to kill yourself and destroy the lady who is your whole life? Why would you curse the day you were ever born, Romeo? Why hurl insults at heaven and earth? These things are all part of your life, and you of theirs.

"You put to shame your body, your heart and your mind if you selfishly waste them like this, rather than use them, as is true and proper, for good purposes. Pull yourself together, young man. Your Juliet is alive, the one for whose love you wanted to kill yourself – a love that you vowed before me to cherish above all things. The law that calls for punishment by death actually became your friend the moment it was turned into exile. For that, you should be overjoyed. So many blessings are being offered to you – happiness in her best aspect seeks only to know what it is you really want, Romeo, yet you pout like a misbehaving child, in spite of the love and good fortune that are yours. Don't you understand that those who deny themselves these things die miserable deaths?

"Go, get yourself to your love as was decreed when you married her. Ascend to her chamber – go in and comfort her as a husband should. But stay no later than five, when the city guards come on duty, for the road to Mantua will be blocked. You can live there until we find time to publicly announce your marriage, let your family and friends know you're safe, and win a full pardon from the Prince, who will then recall you so that you can return, with twenty thousand times more joy than you went away with. Nurse, you go on ahead. Give my greetings to your lady and see that she manages to have the rest of the household get to bed, which their sorrow will incline them to after what's happened today. Tell her Romeo is on his way."

"Good lord, I could stay here all night listening to such wisdom. My, what a wonderful thing learning is. My lord," she says to Romeo, "I'll tell my lady you are coming."

"Thank you," he smiles, "and tell her I'm prepared to be scolded."

Nurse starts to leave but turns back, having remembered something.

"Here sir, a ring she wanted me to give you, sir. Well, I suppose I better be going for it is growing late."

"How well my spirits are revived by this," Romeo declares when Nurse is gone.

"Good. Now remember, be gone before the guards come on duty, and by daybreak be in your disguise and on your way out of town. Stay in Mantua. I'll get in touch with your man there – "

"Balthasar."

"He will keep you informed of how things are progressing here. Give me your hand. It is late. Farewell, my boy. Good night."

"Except that a greater joy calls for me, my grief is brief at having to part from thee. Farewell."

——— ♥ ———

The noble Count Paris has come to meet with Capulet and Lady Capulet about his marriage proposal.

"Unfortunately," Capulet begins, "things have worked out in such a way that we have had no time to discuss matters with our daughter, sir. You must understand, she was extremely fond of her cousin Tybalt, and so was I, in fact. Yet, sad to say, we are all born to die," he remarks gravely. "It's very late. She won't be coming down again tonight. I can assure you that if it hadn't been for your visit I would have been in bed an hour ago."

"These times of woe leave little time to woo," Paris observes. "Lady Capulet, good night. Give my regards to your daughter."

"I will, and early tomorrow I will talk this over with her. Tonight she's simply too overcome with grief."

Paris prepares to leave, but Capulet asks him to wait.

"Sir Paris, I feel I can make you an offer of my child's love. I believe in all honesty I can persuade her to respect my wishes; in fact, I am positive of it. Wife, go to her before you retire, acquaint her with my son Paris's love, and inform her – take notice of this – that next Wednesday – one moment, what day is today?"

"Monday, my lord."

"Monday! Indeed! Well, Wednesday will be too soon, then. Let us say Thursday."

Capulet turns to his wife. "So tell her that Thursday she will marry this noble gentleman. Will you be ready?" he inquires of Paris. "Are you in accord with such hastiness? We won't make a great to-do, there will just be a few of our intimate friends. Otherwise, Tybalt having been so recently slain, it could appear that we are being disrespectful to one of our kinsmen if we hold too elaborate a celebration. Therefore we'll invite about half a dozen friends, no more than that. So, what do you think about Thursday?"

"My lord, I wish that tomorrow was Thursday."

"Well, I guess you should be on your way then. Thursday it shall be. Go in to Juliet on your way to bed, my dear, and tell her to begin preparing for her wedding day. Farewell my lord. – Some light up to my bedroom there! I do declare, it's so late now that we could just as well call it early. Good night."

As dawn begins to break, Romeo rises from Juliet's bed and goes to stand at the window. In a few moments, Juliet awakens and comes over to join him.

"Must you really go?" she asks, putting her arms around him. "It is not daylight yet. It was the nightingale and not the lark that caught your wary ear. She sings every night on the nearby pomegranate tree. Believe me, love, it was the nightingale."

"No, it was the lark," Romeo smiles, "the first bird of morning, not a nightingale. Look at the brightening streaks of light poking through the eastern clouds. Night's candles have melted down, and cheerful day stands tiptoe on the misty mountain tops. I must go and live, or stay and die."

"But the light you see is not daylight, I know it, I do. It is some meteor that the sun has set ablaze to be a torchbearer for you on the road to Mantua. So stay a while longer. You needn't go right now," she murmurs and they kiss.

"Let them capture me, let them put me to death," Romeo says defiantly, "as long as it's what you would like. I'll agree that the distant gray sky is not morning opening its eyes. I'll accept that it is not the lark whose song rises to the vault of heaven high overhead. I have a stronger desire to stay now than to go. Come death, you are welcome to me, since Juliet wills that I remain by her side."

Unsure whether he's teasing or not, Juliet gazes thoughtfully at the morning sky.

There is no doubt that Friar Laurence's deadline is near.

"How are you, my twin soul?" Romeo asks. "We can talk some more. It is not yet day."

"It is, my love," Juliet says, having changed her mind. "I see now that it is. You must get on your way, you must go. It is the lark singing, after all, its harsh discords and unpleasing notes reminding me that we are to be pulled apart, that there will be those out hunting today, but not for their usual prey. It's growing brighter and brighter."

"Brighter and brighter," Romeo whispers, "yet darker and darker our coming woes – "

The Nurse suddenly barges into Juliet's room, frantic about something.

"Madam."

"Nurse?"

"My lady, your mother, is on her way up to see you," she warns. "It's sunrise, be careful, watch yourselves," she tells the two of them and briskly leaves.

"Then, window, let sunrise in and let life out," Juliet tells Romeo. He pauses before going out to the balcony.

"Farewell, my love. One kiss and I'll descend."

They kiss quickly but passionately before Romeo climbs over the railing and goes down.

"Are you gone so soon?" Juliet calls. "My love, my lord, my husband, my friend? I will need to hear from you every hour of every day, for each minute will seem like days – by which count it will be years before I see my Romeo again."

"Farewell," he calls from below. "I will send greetings as often as I can, my love."

"Do you think we will ever meet again?"

"Of course we will! And all our troubles will be pleasant stories we can tell our children in years to come."

"Romeo?"

"My love?"

"I just had a horrible premonition. I thought I saw you, now you are down below, lying dead on the floor of a tomb. Either my eyesight is off, or you look strangely pale."

"Trust me, love, from here you do too. Thirsty farewells consume our blood. Adieu, adieu."

He disappears in the trees behind the garden.

"Oh Fortune, Fortune! People say you are fickle and can change suddenly. But if you are, what lies in store for him who has promised to be faithful? Be fickle, Fortune, for then I can hope you will not keep him long, but send him back soon."

"Good day, daughter, are you up?" Lady Capulet calls from inside the room.

"Who is it?" Juliet answers, perplexed. "It's my lady, my mother! Is she up early or just late going to bed? Strange that she would come to see me like this." She scampers promptly back into her room, runs to her bed and dives under the covers.

"Why, what's this Juliet?"

"I am not feeling well, mother."

"Still weeping for your friend's death. What are you trying to do, wash him from his grave with tears? Even if you could, that wouldn't bring him back to life. My advice is put an end to it: a little grief fulfills your loving obligation, too much only shows a lack of discretion."

"But let me weep for my feelings of loss."

"Weeping for that feeling is not the same as weeping for your friend."

"Feeling the loss so much, I can't help but weep for my friend."

"Well, girl, you are probably not weeping as much for his death as for the fact the villain who slaughtered him remains alive."

"What villain mother?'

"The villain Romeo, of course."

"May you be miles away by now," Juliet says to herself. "May God forgive him. I know I do, with all my heart. And yet no man like he makes my heart grieve."

"That's because the murderous traitor lives."

"Yes, mother, and no two hands would enjoy avenging my cousin's death more than mine."

"We will have our revenge, don't worry. Stop your weeping now. I'll be sending a man to Mantua, where the banished renegade has apparently gone to live, and our man will see to it that a deadly drink will have him keeping company with Tybalt in no time. I hope that will satisfy you."

"I don't believe I will ever be satisfied, mother, till I see him – dead – my poor heart being so distraught over our kinsman. Mother, if you could find a man to bear a poison, I would mix something in – so that Romeo upon taking it would soon be sound asleep. How I hate to hear that name, and yet I cannot go to him and wreak the love I had for my cousin upon the person who killed him."

"If you can find the means, I'll find the man. But for now, I have some wonderful news to tell you."

"And it couldn't come at a better time. What is it you want to tell me, your ladyship?"

"Well now, you know you have a caring father, child, one who to relieve you of your sorrow has arranged a special day, a quite unexpected surprise which even I didn't see coming."

"A special day, mother?"

"Early next Thursday morning, at Saint Peter's Church, the gallant young nobleman Count Paris is looking forward to making you his joyful bride."

"By Saint Peter's Church and Peter too, he will not make me his joyful bride. Why is this being proposed so hastily, that I'm being asked to take a husband who has never even courted me? Please be good enough to tell father that I am not prepared to get married yet. And when I am, I swear it shall be to Romeo, whom you know I hate, rather than Paris. A special day indeed," Juliet says in disappointment, and breaks into tears.

"Your father is on his way up. Tell him yourself and see how he takes it."

Capulet enters his daughter's bedroom, closely attended by the Nurse.

"When the sun sets, the dew begins to fall, but for the sunset of my brother's son, it rains continuously. Have you turned yourself into a water fountain, my girl? Still showering us with your tears? It seems to me in one small body you have gathered a ship, a sea, and a wind, for your eyes are ebbing and flowing like the sea. Your body is the ship, sailing on the salty wave tears, your sad sighs the winds raging over this sea of tears with nothing to calm your tempest-tossed body. And so, wife? Did you tell her about what we have arranged?"

"I did, and she thanks you, but will have none of it. I wish the fool were married to her grave!"

"Just one moment. Help me to hear what you're saying to me. She wants nothing to do with it? She doesn't appreciate the effort we have made on her behalf? She's not pleased? She doesn't thank her lucky stars that, undeserving as she is, we have arranged for her to marry one of the most eligible men in all Verona?"

"Not pleased, father, although thankful in a way, for I could never be pleased with what I hate, but only thankful for hating what you wish me to love."

"What, what, what?" Capulet storms. "What kind of silly logic is this? 'Pleased' and 'thankful' and 'no thank you'? You listen up, miss. Thank me no 'thanks' and please me no 'pleaseds', but have your legs ready next Thursday to walk with Paris into Saint Peter's Church, or I'll drag you there myself. Damn it, you worthless creature! You little hag! You tart!"

"Husband, please, are you out of your mind?"

"Good father," Juliet pleads, "I beg you on my knees, can you wait until you've heard what I have to say?"

"Curse you, you disobedient, good-for-nothing woman! I'll tell you what – you present yourself in that church on Thursday or never look me in the face again. Don't speak to me, don't talk to me, don't utter a single word. I could hit you right now – wife, we often thought how lucky we were to have only one child; but now I see that even one is too much, and that we have been cursed by having her. Good riddance to her shameless stubbornness!"

"God have mercy on her," Nurse remarks timidly, "you should be ashamed for scolding her like that, my lord."

"And why is that my Lady Wisdom? Hold your tongue, you simple creature. Go and gossip with your chatterbox friends."

"I speak no treason, sir, only – "

"Oh good God!"

"May a person speak?"

"No, you mumbling fool! Save your silly nonsense for the gossip circle. We don't need it here."

"You are too angry," Lady Capulet warns her husband.

"God's mercy, it makes me so mad! Day, night, work, play, alone, with other people, I worry constantly about finding her a good husband. Now I've come up with one who just happens to be related to the nobility, is handsome, youthful, of good character – in short the perfect match – and all the girl can do is whine and complain in the face of her good fortune. 'I'm not getting married, I cannot love yet, I am still too young, please forgive me'. If you will not get married, I'll forgive you all right. I'll forgive you for eating somewhere else from now on, for living somewhere else too. Think about that for a minute and remember, I'm not in the habit of joking about such things. Thursday is approaching. Look into your heart. Consider what I'm saying. If you see things my way, I'll give you to my friend. If you refuse to, damn you! Beg! Starve! Die in the streets for all I care. I promise you as well that all that is mine will be of no help to you, of that you can be certain. Think about it, I tell you. I will not be tampered with," Capulet finishes and storms out of the room.

"Is there no pity in the clouds above which can see the depths of my grief? Please dear mother, don't cast me away, put the marriage off for a month, even for a week, but if you don't my bridal bed will be within the tomb where Tybalt lies."

"Don't talk to me, for I won't say a thing. Do what you wish, for I can have nothing more to do with you."

When she is gone, Juliet turns in desperation to Nurse.

"How on earth can I prevent this from happening, Nurse? I already have a husband with whom I've exchanged vows. How can I exchange the same vows with someone else if that husband is still alive? Advise me, tell me what I should do. Why oh why is heaven playing such cruel tricks on someone as innocent as I? What do you think? Have you nothing whatsoever to say? Nothing that would give me the least bit of comfort?"

"Here's what I suggest. Romeo is banished and for nothing in the world would he dare come back to confront you over another marriage – or if he did, it could only be in secret. He would be found out and, well, you know the rest. Things being what they are now, I think it's best you marry Paris. He's a lovely gentleman. Romeo's like an old dish towel compared to him. No eagle has such wings, such sharpness of mind and eye as Paris does. Cross my heart and hope to die, I think you will be happier in this second marriage, for it really does tower over the first. Or even if it doesn't, your first one is as good as dead anyway, since living here you're of no use to Romeo, or he to you, living there."

"Is this spoken from the heart?"

"And from my soul too, or curse the both of them."

"Amen."

"What?"

"Well, you have comforted me a great deal after all, Nurse. Go and tell my mother that, having displeased my father, I have gone to Friar Laurence's cell to make my confession and seek forgiveness."

"I certainly will tell her! It's a wise decision, my dear."

"Damned old woman!" Juliet says, denouncing Nurse. "Treacherous creature! It's just as wrong for her to have me break my wedding vows, as it is to belittle my husband, the same man whose praises she used to sing such a short time ago. From now on I will never confide in her again. I'll talk to Friar Laurence and ask him for his aid. If all else fails, I'll take this life which God has made."

—— ♥ ——

Friar Laurence is taken aback when Paris pays a visit to his cell.

"This Thursday? That's in two days."

"Capulet, my future father-in-law, has requested it."

"You say you aren't sure what the lady thinks about the marriage," the Friar says, pondering what he should advise. "In my experience, worthy Count, that strikes me as unusual. In truth, it makes me quite uneasy," he remarks with a solemn frown.

"She weeps incessantly over Tybalt's death, I've been told, so I haven't pressed her on the topic of love. Venus doesn't enjoy herself in a house of tears, if you know what I mean. Her father now feels it's dangerous the way sorrow has taken over her life, and in his considered opinion a hasty marriage will get her to stop crying, which is partly the result of being by herself both night and day. Capulet feels she needs to meet more people. That's the reason things will have to move so quickly."

"I wish I didn't know why they should be slowed down," Friar Laurence mutters to himself. "But sir, here comes the lady toward my cell."

Indeed, Juliet has arrived to see Friar Laurence.

"I am very happy to see you, my lady and my wife."

"That may be, sir, at such time as I am your wife."

"Not 'may be', love, 'must be', this coming Thursday."

"What must be, will be."

"That is certainly true," Friar Laurence murmurs quietly.

"Have you come to the holy Father for your confession?" Paris asks.

"If I answer that, I would be confessing to you."

"Be sure you let him know that you love me, then."

"I will confess to you that I love him."

"As you will, I'm sure, that you love me," Paris persists.

"If I do so, it will be more worthwhile spoken behind your back in privacy, rather than to your face," Juliet points out.

"Poor thing," says Paris, "your face shows signs of having shed too many tears."

"The tears have gained a small victory in that, although it was unattractive enough before they took their toll."

"You worsen it more than tears with a slander like that," Paris says, scolding her.

"It's not slander, sir, it's the truth," she counters, "and what I said, I said it to my face."

"Your face is mine, and you have slandered it."

"That may be so, for it is not my own – are you free to hear my confession, holy Father, or shall I come back after evening service?"

"I'm free when I want to be, pensive daughter," Friar Laurence allows, "and now is very convenient. – My lord, we must have some time alone."

"God keep me from interfering in someone's devotions. Juliet, as is the custom, my musicians and I will wake you early on Thursday. Until then, adieu, and treasure this holy kiss." Paris presses his lips to her forehead and then departs.

"Shut the door, Father, and when you have, start weeping with me, beyond hope, beyond cure, beyond all help!"

"Dear Juliet, I know what is being planned, and it weighs heavily on my mind. I have heard that you are required – with no chance of postponement – to be married to Count Paris this Thursday."

"Don't tell me you have heard about it Friar, without telling me how I can prevent it. If in your wisdom you can't help me, tell me the wisest thing to do now is use this knife and help myself. God joined my heart to Romeo's, you our hands; but before this hand, fastened as it is to Romeo's, can be joined to another, or my true heart in rebellion against itself can open to another, it will slay both heart and hand. Therefore, from your knowledge of these matters, offer me some wisdom at once, or between me and my suffering, this knife will intervene to provide me with a better solution than years of art and practice. Say something, and quickly. I am longing to die, unless you can offer me a remedy."

"Wait, dear girl! I think there is some hope, even though it means doing something as dangerous as what we are trying to prevent. If, rather than marry Count Paris, you have the strength to want to kill yourself, then it is likely you would undertake something resembling death to avoid this unholy union, something in which you would have to contend with your own death in order to escape from it. If you are willing to risk it, I will give you a remedy."

"Order me to leap from the highest tower rather than marry Paris, or have me pass through a den of thieves, or kiss the fangs of serpents. Bury me in a grave filled with men's bones, rotting flesh, eyeless skulls – I will do anything, without fear or doubt, to remain a faithful wife to the man I truly love."

"Very well, then. Go home, be merry and bright, and agree to marry Paris. Wednesday is tomorrow. Make sure you're alone when you go to bed, don't let Nurse be in the room with you. Once you're in bed, drink the contents of this small glass vial. Your veins will immediately feel cold, you'll fall right to sleep, and your pulse will even stop beating. There will be no signs of life in you – you will have stopped breathing, the pink will disappear from your lips and cheeks so they're as pale as ashes. Your body, cold and stiff, the unblinking stare in your eyes – it will appear as if you have left the world behind. This will continue for forty-two hours, and then you will awake as you would from a pleasant sleep.

"But when the bridegroom comes for you Thursday morning, there you will be, dead. Following our custom, you'll be dressed in your finest clothes, laid on the funeral bier with your seemingly unmarried face uncovered, and carried to the same ancient vault where the Capulets are buried. In the meantime, before you reawaken, I'll send word to Romeo telling him of our plan. He will come here and the two of us will be there when you open your eyes. That night Romeo will take you with him to Mantua, thus freeing you from your plight, provided that no change of heart or wavering spirit weakens your desire to go through with this."

"Give it to me, Father. Give it to me and don't talk to me about fear."

"Here it is. Now, get on your way. May you be strong and unafraid in your resolve. I'll send a friar to Mantua immediately with a letter for your husband."

"Love, give me strength, and strength the help I need. Farewell, dear Father!"

———— ❤ ————

Capulet, Lady Capulet and Nurse are preparing for the wedding celebration. Serving men are coming and going, decorating, moving furniture and setting tables.

"Invite the people whose names are written here," Capulet instructs one of his serving men. "You, fellow," he calls to another, "go and hire twenty of the best cooks."

"You'll have no bad ones, sir, for I'll check to see if they can lick their fingers."

"What? What does that tell you?"

"Believe it or not, sir, a bad cook is afraid to lick his own fingers. Therefore, any cook who doesn't, won't be getting hired by me."

"All right, carry on then. I don't see how we'll be ready for a wedding in time – Nurse, that reminds me, did my daughter go to see Friar Laurence after all?"

"Indeed she did, sir."

"Well, perhaps he talked some sense into her spiteful, headstrong – "

"Hold on, sir," Nurse interrupts, "there she is now, home from confession. And, my word, there's a happy look on the girl's face!"

"Hello, my stubborn one: where have you been idling?" Capulet calls to Juliet.

"Where I've learned to apologize for my willful disobedience in opposing your wishes, father." She walks over to join her parents. "Friar Laurence has instructed me to get down on my knees and humbly seek your pardon. Please forgive me. From now on I will accept your authority without question or complaint." She bows her head and kneels down before him.

"Send word to Count Paris informing him of this," Capulet orders one of his attendants. "I'll have them tie the knot tomorrow morning," he rejoices.

"I met the young man at Friar Laurence's cell and offered my love appropriately, not overstepping the bounds of modesty, father."

"I am glad to hear it, daughter. This is marvellous news. Stand up now, stand up! This is the way it should be between a father and his child. Let me talk to Count Paris. For goodness sake, someone go and fetch him! As God is my witness, our whole city owes a debt of gratitude to this holy Friar."

"Nurse, will you help me sort through my closet to find the proper clothes for a bride to wear tomorrow morning?"

"No, it's not until Thursday," Lady Capulet points out. "We've got plenty of time."

"Go along with her Nurse," Capulet instructs, "we'll have the ceremony tomorrow."

Once Juliet and her Nurse have left, Lady Capulet turns to her husband.

"We won't have nearly enough food, and there's no way of buying more. It's almost night now."

"Don't worry, I will improvise. Everything will be fine, I promise you. Go and help Juliet choose a dress. Leave everything to me, I'm probably not going to bed tonight. I'll play the housewife for once – what's this? All the servants are out? Very well," he sighs. "I'll make the trek across town to see Count Paris myself, let him know the plans have changed and we're arranging things for tomorrow. My heart is wonderfully light, now that Juliet has seen the error of her ways."

Nurse is helping Juliet decide what to wear on her wedding day.

"I think these clothes will suit me best, Nurse," Juliet tells her, admiring the dress she is trying on. "It will do nicely. Thank you. Now, when it's time, I would like to be on my own tonight. There is much praying I need to do so that heaven will smile upon my happy day and forgive my stubborn, wrongful behavior with my father – "

Lady Capulet enters the room to see how things are progressing.

"You two are very busy, do you need any help from me?"

"No, mother, we've selected those items which will be appropriate to the occasion. So if you don't mind, I'd like to be left alone and let Nurse sit up with you tonight, since I am sure you have your hands full with all that has to be done in so short a time."

"Good night, then. Go to bed and get a good sleep. You'll need it."

When Nurse and Lady Capulet have gone, Juliet takes to her bed and readies the small glass vial containing the mixture Friar Laurence gave her.

"God knows when we shall meet again," she says, glancing nervously around her darkened room. "I feel a faint, cold fear rushing through my veins that seems like it's freezing all the warmth inside me. I'll call them back and have them console me – Nurse!" she calls, although not loud enough to be heard. "What would she do? I have to perform this horrible act alone. Come, vial. But what if, what if the mixture doesn't work? Will I have to get married in the morning after all? No, no! This will prevent that from happening," she says, and removes a knife from a drawer in her bedside table. "You lie there," she says, placing the knife beside her on the bed.

"Yet, what if it's a poison which the Friar prepared so I really would die, because he would be disgraced if it came to light he had already married me to Romeo? I'm afraid it could be. Perhaps he – but I don't see that a man as revered for his holiness as the Friar would do something like that. Or what if I wake up in the tomb before Romeo comes to rescue me? What a terrifying thought. Wouldn't I be trapped inside the vault without fresh air, and possibly suffocate before Romeo comes? Or if I did stay alive, wouldn't the deathly dark terrors of the place, the tomb where the bones of my ancestors have been buried for hundreds of years – where Tybalt's bloody corpse now lies festering in its shroud – where, too, they say in the dead of night evil spirits lurk – and the loathsome smells, the hideous sounds. And driven mad by these horrible fears attacking me, might I not start searching through my forefathers' skeletons, even Tybalt's mangled body, until I found some great kinsman's bone I could use as a club to dash out my own desperate brains? Even now I think I can see my cousin's ghost looking for Romeo who stuck his body on the spit of his rapier's point! Stop, Tybalt, stop! Romeo, Romeo, Romeo, here's the cure! I drink to thee!"

She swallows the Friar's poison and collapses on her bed, the sudden movement ruffling the four-poster curtains for a brief moment before they come to rest around her lifeless body.

—— ♥ ——

Though it's the middle of the night, Lady Capulet and the Nurse are still busy supervising the cooks and servants who are working arduously to prepare the upcoming wedding feast.

"Wait, take these keys and fetch more spices," Lady Capulet tells the Nurse.

"They're calling for dates and pears in the pastry room, m'am," Nurse replies.

Capulet hurries in and takes stock of the situation.

"Come along, everyone. Move, move, move! The rooster has already crowed twice. They'll be ringing the three o'clock bell before you know it. See to the pastries, good Angelica – and don't worry about the expense."

"You know what they say can happen with too many cooks, sir," Nurse reminds Capulet. "Why don't you go to bed. My word, you'll make yourself sick for tomorrow staying up this late."

"No, not a bit. Why, I've stayed awake on less important occasions than this and never had to deal with the ill effects."

"Oh, but that was chasing women, sir. I'm the one doing the chasing now!"

"You're quite the character, Nurse. Quite the character!"

As Lady Capulet and the Nurse retire, they pass three serving men toting iron roasting spits, logs for the fire, and large, round wicker baskets.

"What's all this, fellow?"

"Things for the cook, sir, I'm not sure what," replies one of the serving men.

"Well hurry then, hurry! You there, bring drier logs! Ask Peter to show you where they are."

"I have a head, sir. I think I can find logs without asking Peter."

"Ah, well said you rascal. You're a loghead then!" Capulet jokes. "Goodness me!" he exclaims, "it's nearly day. Paris will be here with his musicians, as promised. My goodness, I think I hear them!"

The sounds of a lute, mandolin and a drum drift through the house, Nurse arriving back in the downstairs hall to see what else needs to be done.

"Go and wake Juliet," Capulet says. "Help her get dressed while I go and chat with Paris. Hurry up, time's a wasting! The bridegroom is here already. Hurry up I say!"

— ♥ —

Several minutes later, Nurse bustles through the door into Juliet's room.

"My lady! Juliet! Still sound asleep are you?"

She parts the curtains around the four-poster bed and peers down at Juliet. "Why, shame on you, sleepyhead! Come along, sweetheart, you're about to become a bride! What, not a word? I suppose you do have to get your sleep in now. Sleep for a week, I say, for tonight Count Paris will make sure you don't get much at all! Oh, God forgive me," she giggles and crosses herself. "My, this is a deep sleep. I guess I'll have to shake you. Madam, madam, madam! I should let Count Paris near the bed – I know *that* would get you moving. You're not going to budge? Hmm, you got up and put your clothes on, then went back to bed again? I have to wake you up, dear. Lady!" She waits a moment. "Lady!" she repeats and shakes Juliet harder. "Lady!" Now it dawns on her that something is very wrong. "My goodness! Oh my goodness!" she cries out in alarm. "Help! Help! My lady's dead! Oh curse the day I was ever born – My Lord! My Lady!"

Lady Capulet enters quickly and joins Nurse at the side of the bed.

"What's all this racket?"

"Oh tragic day!"

"What's going on?"

"Look! Look!" Nurse chokes out the words.

"Oh me, oh me!" Lady Capulet gasps. "My child, my only life. Look at me, say something or I will die too. Help! Help! Call for help!" Tears streaming down her face, she tries to rouse Juliet.

Lord Capulet strides into the room in a huff.

"For goodness sake," he declares impatiently, "bring Juliet downstairs, her husband is here."

"She's dead!" Nurse informs him. "She has died in the night! She's dead!"

"Oh sorrowful, sorrowful day!" Lady Capulet moans. "She's dead. My daughter is dead!" She rocks Juliet's limp body in her arms.

"Wait, let me see her. Step aside and – she's cold, there's no pulse, her limbs are stiff. Her lips have no life in them – death covers her like an early frost upon the sweetest flower in all the fields," he says in utter disbelief.

"Oh mournful day!" the Nurse wails.

"Oh tragic, tragic time!" Lady Capulet sobs.

"Death has taken her to punish me; my tongue won't move, I cannot speak."

Friar Laurence now arrives, with Paris and his band of musicians.

"So, is our bride ready to go to church?" Friar Laurence inquires.

"Ready to go, but never to return. Oh son," Capulet says to Paris, "Death has taken your wife during the night. There she lies, flower that she was, deflowered by him. Death is now my son-in-law, Death has become my heir," he says gravely. "My daughter has married him. When I die, I will leave him everything. Life, living, it all goes to Death."

"I have waited so long for this morning to arrive," Paris says sadly, "and now it greets me with a sight like this."

Lady Capulet struggles as she speaks. "Cursed, unhappy, wretched, detested day. The most miserable hour that time has seen on its neverending journey. My poor and loving child, the one thing I could rejoice and take comfort in, and here cruel Death has snatched her away from me for good."

"There has never been a darker day than this," Nurse moans. "Woeful, woeful, woeful day."

"Deceived, divorced, wronged, spited, slain," Paris says somberly. "Despicable Death, you have betrayed us, ruined us in the cruelest of all possible ways. Oh love! Oh life!" he declares looking down at Juliet. "No longer alive, but my love always will be."

"Despised, despairing, hated, martyred, killed," Capulet says, echoing Paris.

"Why did you choose this unfortunate time to come and murder, murder what was to have been the most joyful occasion? My child, my soul, you are dead. Alas, my child is dead, and with her my joys are now buried."

"Silence, all of you," Friar Laurence says sternly. "The cure for a catastrophe like this won't be found in noisy outcries and harsh denunciations. Heaven above and all of you here shared the life of this young girl; now only heaven does, but what could be better for the girl? The parts of her each of you had, could not keep her from dying, but heaven will do his part and keep her throughout eternity." He glares at Capulet. "What you sought for her was a higher station in society; your own idea of heaven was to see yourself move up in the world through her. Above the clouds? As high as heaven itself? Through your ambition, your desire for lofty status, you gave up everything in order to join the upper ranks. Such a marriage would not have been good even if it lasted for years. In a marriage such as that, it's best for a girl if she dies young. Dry your tears, place rosemary on her body as is customary. Dress her in her finest clothes and carry her to the church. Though at such times nature inclines us to be sad, reason finds our tears merely an excuse to be glad."

"Take what we've prepared for a celebration and turn it into preparation for a funeral," Capulet says. "Have the instruments give way to the tolling of the bells, our wedding banquet to a burial meal, our hymns of praise to soft, sullen dirges, the bridal flowers to coffin sprays."

"Sir, madam, Sir Paris," Friar Laurence instructs, "leave now and prepare to follow Juliet's body to the churchyard. The heavens have frowned upon you once for doing wrong; do not annoy them again, for their will can be as harsh as it is strong."

When the others have left, bearing Juliet away, Nurse and the musicians remain behind.

"Good," says one, "we can pack up our cases and go home."

"Your cases indeed," says the Nurse. "This is one of the most pitiful cases you're ever likely to see."

"Isn't that the truth," the musician jokes, "a case that's now closed."

But the feeble humor is wasted on Nurse, who has already left. In her place she has sent Peter, the servant who assists her, to deal with the musicians.

"Musicians, musicians! Give us a version of 'Heart's ease'. Play 'Heart's ease' and you will make my day."

"Why 'Heart's ease?" the musician Simon Catling wants to know.

"Because," Peter replies, "my heart is playing 'I'm so very sad'. Play me some merry down in the dumps music, as they say."

"As they say, there's no such thing," says Hugh Rebeck.

"So you won't?"

"We can't!" says Simon.

"Then I'll give you what's coming to you."

"And what would that be?"

"Not money, that's for sure. More likely one of my fingers. The royal finger."

"I'll give you the slave treatment then."

"Then I'll apply the slave's stick to your head. I'll *re* you, I'll *fah* you. Do you note what I'm saying?"

"You can *re* us and *fa* us, if you can catch us."

"Put away your stick and take out your wit, if you catch my meaning."

"Very well, wit it shall be. Answer this question. 'When crippling grief the heart does wound, And doleful dumps the mind oppress, Then music with her silver jingle' – what comes next? Why is it 'Music with her silver jingle'? Simon Catling?"

"Because silver has a sweet sound would be my guess."

"Not even close," Peter tells him. "What say you, James

Soundpost?"

"Uh, I don't really know," says slow-moving James.

"Oh, for heaven's sake. You're the singer here. I'll tell you. It's 'Music with her silver jingle' because musicians have no gold to jingle in their pockets. Don't you see? 'Then music with her silver jingle, With speedy help relieves distress.'" He walks away proudly with his chin in the air.

"What a pesky fool that man is."

"String him up, the scoundrel. All right, we'll go in here, wait for the mourners, then stay for supper."

"But will I have to sing for my supper?" James Soundpost wonders.

—— ♥ ——

5.1

In Mantua, Romeo bides his time waiting for word from Friar Laurence about the situation in Verona.

"If I can believe what my dreams are telling me, I should be receiving some news from Verona. Today I've been feeling strangely light-hearted, like I'm floating gently a few feet off the ground. I dreamt that Juliet arrived here and found me dead – a strange dream that was upsetting, except she brought me back to life again with a kiss, and when I awoke I was an emperor." He smiles to himself. "How strong love is when only dreaming about it has such powerful effects."

A short while later he looks up when he notices Balthasar, his servant, galloping toward him on horseback. In a moment he dismounts and waits to catch his breath.

"News from Verona!" Romeo rejoices. "How are you Balthasar – did you bring me letters from the Friar? How is my mother? Is my father well? How is Juliet? Most important of all, how is she? Nothing can be amiss if she is well."

"Then she is well and nothing can be amiss," Balthasar reports uncomfortably, "because her body is lying in the Capulet tomb, and her eternal soul lives with the angels. I saw her laid out in the vault myself and came as fast as I could to tell you. Pardon me for bringing such awful news, but I felt I had to do my duty, sir."

"Is it really so?" Romeo cries in dismay. "Then I have no choice. You know where I live, Balthasar."

"Yes, sir."

"Bring me a pen and some paper. And hire the fastest horses. I will leave tonight."

"Are you sure that's a good idea, sir? You've turned white as a ghost and there's a crazed look in your eyes. I'm afraid you'll do something drastic, sir."

"I'm fine, Balthasar. Believe me. Just leave me be and do what I asked you to. You really don't have letters for me from the Friar?"

"No, my lord."

"Well, it doesn't matter. Off you go. And hire the horses. I'll be along shortly."

Romeo watches Balthasar ride away and then lets his eyes sweep over the horizon. In a daze and near tears, he starts walking.

"Well, Juliet, I will lie with you tonight if I can only figure out how. But desperate deeds come easily to mind for desperate men – I remember noticing an apothecary living nearby. He was gathering herbs, dressed in ragged clothes, with thick, over-hanging eyebrows, a gaunt face and a grim, down-turned mouth. It looked as if poverty and misery had worn him to the bone. His dreary little shop was crammed with dried fish, animal skins, dead tortoises, and he even had a stuffed alligator hanging over dusty shelves littered with all kinds of junk. I remember thinking at the time that if a man ever needed poison, which the penalty for possessing is death, this destitute old wretch would be just the one to sell him some. If I recall, that is his house over there. Because of the holiday, the shop might be closed. Hello! Apothecary? Hello!"

In a few moments the apothecary opens his door a crack and peers out at Romeo.

"Who is yelling for me?"

"A word with you, fellow," says Romeo. "I see you have difficulty making ends meet. Here's forty gold ducats if you'll let me have a dram of poison, something powerful enough to kill someone instantly – something that will hit like a cannon from close range."

"I have such deadly drugs, but the law in Mantua forbids me to dispense them on pain of death."

"Is a man as poor and destitute as you afraid of death? The world is not your friend, nor the world's laws. But I can be by offering you this."

5.2

The apothecary stares suspiciously at the small fortune of gold coins in Romeo's hand.

"I don't agree with this, but my dire poverty will accept your offer." He takes Romeo's money.

"Don't worry, friend. I am paying you for your poverty; agreement has nothing to do with it."

Romeo steps in when the man opens the door. Rummaging on his shelves, the apothecary soon returns with a small bottle.

"Put this in any liquid you wish and drink it all at once. If you had the strength of twenty men it would finish you off in the blink of an eye."

"Here is your gold – a worse poison to the human soul, causing more murder in this cruel world than all the mixtures you could ever concoct. I'm selling you poison, my friend, you have sold me none. Farewell, buy some food, put on some weight. Come, simple liquid – I can't think of you as poison – and go with me. We will descend to Juliet's grave, and there I will use thee."

♥

Friar John arrives in Verona from Mantua to see Friar Laurence at his cell.

"Are you home Brother Franciscan?"

"I know that voice – Friar John! Welcome from Mantua. How is young Romeo? Did you bring me a letter from him?"

"I found a barefoot brother of ours to accompany me to Verona as required in our Order, but he was visiting in a house where authorities suspected there might have been some infection from the plague, so we were kept confined longer than expected, which delayed our departure from Mantua."

"Who took my letter to Romeo then?"

"I couldn't send it, nor find anyone who was able to leave town because of the plague. Here it is, I've brought it back with me."

"This is such horrible bad luck. In faith, the letter was no simple matter but one of urgent importance. The fact it didn't reach him could have disastrous consequences. Go quickly, Friar John, find me an iron bar and bring it straight back here."

"I'm on my way, Brother Laurence," Friar John says obligingly, recognizing how serious the situation might be.

"I must go to the tomb alone," Friar Laurence says. "Juliet will be awake in less than three hours. She will curse me for not getting word to Romeo about all that has happened – I must send another to Mantua and keep her here until he comes. Poor girl, buried alive in a tomb full of the dead."

Paris and a pageboy emerge from the darkness in the churchyard and creep quietly toward the Capulet family tomb with flowers, a small jar of holy water, and a torch.

"Hand me the torch, boy. I'll have to put it out. Go and stand over there, out of sight under the yew trees, and keep an ear to the ground in case someone comes. Signal me with a whistle if anyone approaches. Give me the flowers. Now do as I said."

The pageboy obeys but is reluctant to go into the darkness under the trees. "I am frightened being left alone here in the churchyard. I think I should wander back until he's done."

Paris meanwhile places flowers around the entrance to the tomb.

"It's fitting I should be adorning your bridal bed with flowers, my sweet flower. Yet how sad it is the canopy under which you now lie is all dust and stone, which I will sprinkle with holy water each night, or if I have none, then with tears distilled by my grieving moans. The funeral respects I pay to your memory I vow to observe nightly, bringing flowers to your grave and weeping for what might have been."

His page suddenly whistles from across the churchyard.

"Someone's coming. Who would be wandering here this late at night? Interrupting my prayers and true love's rite? Carrying a torch as well? I'll slip into the darkness for a bit."

Romeo and Balthasar make their way toward the tomb with a torch, a pickaxe and an iron bar.

"Hand me the pickaxe and the wrenching iron. This letter I need you to take to my father first thing in the morning. Give me the light. Now, I order you, upon your life, that no matter what you see or hear, do not try to stop me. Why I'm going into this place of death is partly to glimpse this lady's face for the last time, but chiefly it's to remove a ring from her finger which I have need of. If you start to worry about what I'm doing and return to spy on me, I swear I will tear you limb from limb, Balthasar. My intentions are savage, wild, and more fierce and unstoppable than ravenous tigers or a storming sea."

"I will be gone, sir, and not trouble you."

"Thank you for being a friend. Take these coins. Live and prosper well in your life. Farewell, good fellow."

He helps Romeo break open the door of the tomb and then moves off into the darkness.

"Just the same, I'm going to hide nearby; I'm afraid for him and what he's going to try."

"Detestable mouth, despicable womb of death," Romeo says as he prepares to enter the eerie tomb. "Devouring the most precious morsel earth has to offer. Watch as I force your rotten jaws to open and, in spite, cram your throat with my body to satisfy your monstrous appetite."

Just as he is stepping forward into the tomb, Paris appears behind him.

"This is that vicious, banished Montague who murdered my dear love's cousin – which caused her such grief she died from it – and here he is, come to do something shameful to their dead bodies."

He rushes for Romeo and confronts him.

"Cease this unholy sacrilege vile Montague. What vengeance can you possible want to inflict on the dead? Guilty man, I arrest you. Do as I say and come with me to the authorities, for you must die."

"Yes I must, and that is why I am here. Good man, do not provoke a desperate soul. Flee from here and leave me to my business. Think about those who have passed away. Let them be a warning to you – don't put another crime on my conscience by arousing my anger. Please go. As heaven is my witness I love you more than myself. Do not stay here, be gone, live and afterwards say it was a mad man's mercy that let me escape."

"I reject such excuses and arrest you as a felon here and now," Paris declares as he takes out his sword.

"You really wish to provoke me, man? Then so be it! Take your life in your hands!"

He draws his weapon and clashes with Paris, whose pageboy is looking on in fear.

"I must go and alert the night guards – "

The fierce fighting continues for several minutes until Romeo, narrowly avoiding a violent thrust from Paris's sword, plunges his own into the man's chest.

Paris falls to the ground, fatally wounded.

"Oh, I am slain! If you have any mercy, open the tomb and lay me with Juliet."

In despair, Romeo can only stand and watch as Paris slowly dies.

"I swear I will do that for you. But let me see your face."

He crouches down and recognizes who it is.

"Mercutio's kinsman, Count Paris! What did Balthasar say as we were riding, when my thoughts were elsewhere and I wasn't really listening – was it that Paris was supposed to marry Juliet? Did he tell me that or did I just dream it? Or did hearing him talk of Juliet drive me mad and only make me think it was so? Oh give me your hand, sir, a man whose story, like my own, is written in misfortune's bitter book."

He takes Paris's body and heads into the Capulet tomb.

"I'll bury you in a triumphant grave. A grave? Oh no, slaughtered friend, this room has a radiance about it, for there lies Juliet, and her beauty turns this place into the brightest feasting hall, shimmering with light.

He sets Paris's body down beside one of the stone tombs.

"Dead soul, you lie there, buried by a dead man. How often when men are at the point of death they become merry, what in the prisons they call 'lightning before death'. Yet how can I call this a lightening? Oh my love, my wife, death that has sucked out the honey of your breath has not yet had the power to affect your beauty. It has not been destroyed. Beauty's flag still flies crimson red in your lips and on your cheeks. Death has not planted its pale flag there. Tybalt, is that you lying in your bloody sheet? What better favor can I do you than let the hand that cut you down in life, take his who was your enemy. Forgive me, cousin.

"As for you, dear Juliet, how can you have remained so fair? Should I believe that intangible Death is amorous? That the lean and hungry monster keeps you here in the dark to be his lover? Fearing that is so, I think it's best if I stay with you and never depart from this dimly lit palace of night again. I will remain right here, with the same worms that wait upon you. Here is where I will stay forever, and shake off life's burdens from my world weary shoulders. Eyes, look one last time. Arms, have your last embrace. And lips, you doors of breath, seal with a righteous kiss an everlasting bargain with Death, who inherits all. Come, bitter conductor, come foul-smelling guide, desperate captain send my seasick weary boat crashing into the rocks at last! Here's to my love!" he cries as he drinks the poison down.

"Oh good apothecary, your drug is quick. Thus, with a kiss, I die."

His lips fall away from Juliet's, and he collapses on the ground beside her.

Outside, carrying a lantern, an iron bar and a spade, barefoot Friar Laurence moves as fast as he can through the churchyard.

"Saint Francis, help me to get to her in time," he says as he hits his foot on a grave stone. "How many times must I trip – who's there?"

"A friend who knows you well, father."

"Balthasar, bless you, son. Tell me, whose torch is that burning over by the Capulet's tomb?"

"It belongs to my master, sir."

"Who?"

"Romeo."

"How long has he been there?"

"About a half an hour, I'd say, sir."

"Come along then."

"I can't, sir. My master thinks I've left. He said he'd kill me if I stayed to see what he was doing."

"Very well, I'll go in alone then. I have a horrible feeling that something's gone wrong."

"As I rested under these yew trees, I thought I saw my master and another man fighting, but my master killed the other man."

"Romeo!" Friar Laurence calls in a frenzy. Near the Capulet tomb he stoops and looks at the two bloody weapons. "No, no, whose blood is this which stains the stony entrance of this burial ground? What does it mean that two gory swords without their owners are lying in this place of peace?"

He makes his way hurriedly into the tomb.

"Oh, what a sight! Romeo! Who else? Paris too? And covered in blood? What ghastly twist of fate could have led to something as horrible as this? The lady stirs."

Dazed and disoriented,, Juliet slowly opens her eyes and looks up at Friar Laurence.

"Oh comforting Father, where is my lord?" she asks softly. "I remember where I am, but was he not to be here as well? Where is my Romeo?"

"I hear noise outside – come, my girl," he says with tender urgency, "we must leave this cave of death, contagion, and monstrous sleep at once! A power greater than ourselves has thwarted our plan. Come, come away! Your husband lies dead by your side, and Paris too. Come and I'll take you to stay with the good sisters at the abbey. There's no time to talk, the night guards are on their way. Come good Juliet. We dare not delay."

"You go, Father. I want to stay."

Torn, Friar Laurence realizes he can't be caught here in the tomb, and runs out.

Juliet struggles to sit up and gazes at Romeo.

"What's this? A cup enclosed in my true love's hand? Poison, I see, has been his timeless end. Oh, you rude fellow. Drunk all, and left no friendly drop for me? I will kiss your lips then. Perhaps some poison lingers there to make me die with its cordial power."

She kisses him tenderly.

"Your lips are still warm!"

The night guards can be heard yelling outside the tomb.

"More noise? Then I'll be brief. Oh happy dagger, come out of your sheath; thrust there – and let me die."

She stabs herself and falls on Romeo.

Paris's pageboy approaches the doors of the Capulet tomb with a band of night guards.

"This is the place. Over there, where the torch is burning."

"The ground is covered in blood," a night guard says. "Search the churchyard. Some of you go, arrest anyone you find."

A group of guards hastens off as ordered, while the others make their way into the burial crypt.

"What a dreadful sight! Here is the dead Count Paris, Juliet just dead, her blood still warm though she's been lying here dead for two days now. Go and tell the Prince. Run to the Capulets, wake the Montagues. Others, have a look around. We see the ground where these victims now reside, but the real grounds for why such a tragedy took place only further details will provide."

One of the night guards brings Balthasar in.

"Here's Romeo's man. We found him in the churchyard."

"Hold him until the Prince arrives."

Another guard brings Friar Laurence into the crypt.

"Here is a friar we found sobbing, moaning and weeping. We took this pickaxe and spade from him as he was sneaking out of the churchyard."

"A serious suspect, it looks like. Hold him as well."

It's not long before the Prince makes his way into the tomb, followed by his entourage.

"What misfortune has taken place which gets out of bed this early in the morning?" he demands, as Lord Capulet, Lady Capulet and their servants gather in the tomb as well. "What is it that's being shouted through the streets?"

"People are crying out 'Romeo'," Lady Capulet says, "some 'Juliet', some 'Paris', and crowds of people are running here toward our family tomb."

"What is the reason for all this?" the Prince asks again.

"Sovereign Prince," a night guard explains, "here lie the dead Count Paris, Romeo, and Juliet – who died recently, but appears to have been killed just now, her blood still strangely warm."

"Find out how these heinous murders took place," the Prince orders.

"We have a friar and Romeo's man in custody," a night guard

explains, "both with tools that were used to open up the tomb."

"Oh good God! Oh wife, look at how our daughter has bled to death. This dagger has been taken from a Montague's sheath and sheathed in her chest by mistake."

"Oh me! This wretched sight will kill me," Lady Capulet laments, unaware that the Montague family and their servants have begun filing into the tomb.

"Come Montague," the Prince says, "you and your wife behold your son and heir, cut down in his prime."

"Alas, my wife passed away last night from grief over her exiled son. I'm afraid to know what further sorrow awaits me here."

"Look and you will see."

"Oh, you unmannerly child," he groans. "How disrespectful to go to your grave before your father"

"Hold back from expressing your further grief and outrage, one and all, until we can sort out the details of what really happened here, and why. Then I will lead you in your grief myself. In the meantime, let patience help to soothe your misfortune. Bring me the individuals who are suspect in these crimes."

"I am the main one," Friar Laurence admits, "although least likely to have committed these horrendous murders, being elsewhere at the time. I stand before you to accuse and acquit myself, however."

"Then tell us what you know," the Prince commands.

"I will be brief, for I don't have long to live myself. Romeo, who's lying there dead, was the husband of Juliet, and she his faithful wife. I married them, and their secret wedding day was Tybalt's doomsday, whose death banished the new bridegroom from this city. It was for him, not for Tybalt, that Juliet fell into despair. You, to put an end to her grief, were arranging for her to marry Paris as soon as humanly possible. Then she came to me and in desperation asked for a means whereby she could avoid this second marriage, otherwise she vowed to kill herself. As one learned in the art of medicines, I gave her a sleeping potion, which had its intended effect of making it look as though she had died.

"In the meantime, I wrote to Romeo telling him he should come here tonight and take her out of the tomb about the time the potion was wearing off. But the man who took my letter, Friar John, was detained in Mantua and returned the letter to me, unopened, last night. I came here on my own when I knew Juliet would be waking up, hoping to take her from the tomb and keep her secretly at my cell till I could arrange to send her to be with Romeo. But when I arrived, shortly before the time of her awakening, there lay Paris and Romeo, both dead. She woke up, I begged her to leave with me and be patient until things worked out, but the noise of people coming made me decide to leave, and she, in desperate straits, would not go because, as we now know, she had decided to end her life. This is all I know. Her Nurse is aware of the marriage, and whatever in this miscarriage of justice is my fault, I am willing to pay for with my life."

"We will always hold you as a holy man," the Prince replies. "Where is Romeo's man? What can he tell us about this?"

"I brought my master news of Juliet's death and then he came straight from Mantua to the tomb here. He asked me to give this letter to his father, and threatened to kill me if I went in the vault after him. He went in, I ran to call the night guards."

After perusing the letter, the Prince addresses the gathering.

"This letter bears out the Friar's words. It describes the course of their love, news of her death, and explains how Romeo bought the poison from a poor apothecary he would use to kill himself here in the tomb, with his beloved Juliet. Where are these two enemies, Capulet and Montague? See what a punishment has been exacted for your mutual hatred, that the heavens have found a way to kill your greatest joys through the love of these your children? And I, for turning a blind eye to your relentless rancor, have lost a pair of kinsmen myself. Everyone has been punished."

"Oh brother Montague," Capulet says, "take my hand. This is my daughter's dowry, I have nothing greater to give."

"I will offer something more," Montague replies as he gives Capulet his hand, "by raising a statue of her in pure gold, so that as long as Verona is known by that name, there will be no monument whose value is set, greater than that of true, and faithful, Juliet."

"In rich gold too, Romeo shall stand by his wife," Capulet declares, "poor sacrifices to our sad and sorrowful strife."

"A gloomy peace this morning brings: the sun in sorrow will not show his head. Go forth to talk of these sad things. Some will be pardoned, and some punished, for never was there a story of such woe, as this of Juliet and her Romeo." ♥

The Shakespeare Novels

Spring 2006

Hamlet
King Lear
Macbeth
Midsummer Night's Dream
Othello
Romeo and Juliet
Twelfth Night

Spring 2007

As You Like It
The Merchant of Venice
Measure for Measure
Much Ado About Nothing
The Taming of the Shrew
The Tempest

www.crebermonde.com

Shakespeare Graphic Novels

Fall 2006

Hamlet
Macbeth
Othello
Romeo and Juliet

www.shakespearegraphic.com

New Directions

The Young and the Restless: *Change*
The Human Season: *Time and Nature*
Eyes Wide Shut: *Vision and Blindness*
Cosmos: *The Light and The Dark*
Nothing But: *The Truth in Shakespeare*
Relationscripts: *Characters as People*
Idol Gossip: *Rumours and Realities*
Wherefore?? *The Why in Shakespeare*
Upstage, Downstage: *The Play's the Thing*
Being There: *Exteriors and Interiors*
Dangerous Liaisons: *Love, Lust and Passion*
Iambic Rap: *Shakespeare's Words*
P.D.Q.: *Problems, Decisions, Quandaries*
Antic Dispositions: *Roles and Masks*
The View From Here: *Public vs. Private Parts*
3D: *Dreams, Destiny, Desires*
Mind Games: *The Social Seen*
Vox: *The Voice of Reason*

Paul Illidge is a novelist and screenwriter who taught high school English for many years. He is the creator of *Shakespeare Manga*, the plays in graphic novel format, and author of the forthcoming *Shakespeare and I*. He is currently working on *Shakespeare in America*, a feature-film documentary. Paul Illidge lives with his three children beside the Rouge River in eastern Toronto.